STAR WARS™

A NEW HOPE

THE PRINCESS,

THE SCOUNDREL,

AND

THE FARM BOY

AN ORIGINAL RETELLING OF

STAR WARS: A NEW HOPE

ALEXANDRA BRACKEN

EGMONT

We bring stories to life

First published in Great Britain 2019
by Egmont UK Limited, The Yellow Building,
1 Nicholas Road, London W11 4AN

© & ™ 2019 Lucasfilm Ltd.

ISBN 978 1 4052 9470 6
70466/001

Printed in UK

To find more great *Star Wars* books, visit
www.egmont.co.uk/starwars

For Dad, who opened up

a whole galaxy of wonder and possibility

AUTHOR'S NOTE

———————————— ✪ ————————————

WHEN YOU MEET another *Star Wars* fan, the same question always comes up: when was the first time you watched the movies? I know exactly when it was for me: Father's Day, 1992. Dad got to decide which movie we'd watch together as a family and, for some reason, decided to pull out an old VHS of *A New Hope*.

I was five. I could not figure out what was happening and why everyone was running around. But I still remember, with perfect clarity, the first time I saw Darth Vader stride on board the *Tantive IV*, his cloak sweeping out behind him, music booming from our television speakers like thunder. I was terrified, but I was also in awe. The fights, the characters, the spaceships – it was like riding a roller coaster without ever leaving the couch.

And once I had a seat on that ride, I never got off.

See, my dad decided a year later that he wanted to start collecting the old toys, posters, and memorabilia from the '70s and '80s from right when the films were released in theatres. Every weekend, the family would pile into our minivan and go to antique shows looking for old figurines, posters, even ceramic mugs of the characters' heads. We went to every major *Star Wars* convention. At one point, Dad was on a first-name basis with half the employees at our local Toys "R" Us. It was our family project, something we did together. It was us.

I was so wrapped up in that universe that from age ten to twelve, all I was interested in reading was *Star Wars* novels. Nothing else seemed to hold my attention. So you can imagine how excited I was (understatement of the millennium) to be asked to write an adaptation of *A New Hope* for young readers, to retell the classic story from a new angle. *The Empire Strikes Back* is full of dark stakes and juicy family drama, and *Return of the Jedi* brings everything full circle. But *A New Hope* is more than the film that launched me into a galaxy far, far away; it's *also* the one that made me interested in storytelling in the first place. It was my first step into a much larger world.

Star Wars so perfectly captures the classic hero's journey. The moment I figured that out, it electrified the story and characters for me in a whole new way, and I had something to study and observe. As a budding teen writer, someone who mostly dabbled in cringe-worthy poetry, this was huge. In fact, I didn't figure out how to write fiction, and that I even *wanted* to write my own original stories, until I tried my hand at writing *Star Wars* fan fiction (all of which is still online over a decade later, as I have tragically forgotten my password and can't log on to the site to delete it).

As a writer, what comes first and foremost for me is always the characters. This, too, is because of *Star Wars* and the emotional impact it had on a very impressionable five-year-old me. In *A New Hope*, we're given a cast of characters who, at first glance, seem to be simple archetypes. The young hero. The rogue. The princess in need of saving. The sidekicks. The wise man. But the older I got, the more complex the characters' motivations became to me – the more I understood how closely *Star Wars* is tied to the idea of family. Not just the Skywalkers but the family Luke, Leia, Han, and the others found in one another, coming from incredibly different backgrounds to work together towards a common goal: hope. In the end, they needed one another – and this struggle – to see exactly what they were made of. By zooming in on Leia's, Han's, and finally Luke's perspective, I got to play with the idea of labels – *princess, scoundrel, farm boy* – and show that these three were so much more than what others, and even they themselves, believed they could be.

I'm still stuck on the idea of family and the importance it plays not only in the scope of the story but in our community of fans around the world. This story binds us together, and it continues to be passed down from one generation to the next – kind of like a cultural heirloom. And in so many ways, *Star Wars* is the story of my family, too. That's never changed, even since my dad lost his battle to cancer a few years ago. We are all connected to this universe, and watching the films or even just thinking about that first time our family watched *A New Hope* together is enough for us to feel close to my dad.

And if that's not the true power of the Force, then I don't know what is.

One final note: for this adaptation, I pulled directly from three sources: my imagination, George Lucas' film script, and Brian Daley's masterful 1981 radio drama script. My thanks to Lucasfilm for their permission to weave all of this material together and for the oppertunity to bring my own vision of the classic story to life.

ALEXANDRA BRACKEN

INTRODUCTION

———————— ☉ ————————

THIS STORY BEGINS as so many do: a long, long time ago . . . in a place far beyond the glittering stars you see in your night sky.

In the time of the Old Republic, hundreds of star systems lived together in peace and prosperity, protected by an ancient order of warriors, the Jedi. But a tide of darkness swept through the galaxy, as unstoppable as it was terrifying, wiping out even the most powerful fighters. Now an evil empire rules the stars, slowly extinguishing the last traces of light and hope in its crushing grip.

Despite the odds, a spark of rebellion lives on. Having won their first victory against the Empire, the Rebels turn their attention to reports of a weapon powerful enough to destroy planets – and obliterate any last hope for freedom.

But, as you well know, heroes emerge from the most unlikely places, at the most unexpected times. This is a story of destiny. Of being in the wrong place at the right time. Of courage. And, yes, of a force more powerful than imagination.

But it is also the story of a princess, a scoundrel and a farm boy. No, there's so much more to them than that. Perhaps they will surprise you. Perhaps they will surprise themselves.

Perhaps they are the heroes the galaxy has needed all along.

——THE——
PRINCESS

CHAPTER ONE

———————— ✪ ————————

LEIA WASN'T THE GIRL they thought she was. That girl might have seen this plan through successfully. The crew of the *Tantive IV* thought Senator Leia Organa would be able to get them untangled from the net she'd flown them straight into. But her plan had gone wrong – so, so wrong. There wasn't any way out, any way to save them. She had let them down, and now there was only one hope for completing her mission.

Leia had never been inside the access corridors on the ship. They were meant for droids and technicians to get around without being trampled underfoot by the crew. Her heart thundered in time with her boots as she ran, and she was sure she'd never find the labour pool. The dull metal corridors and paths were lit by only a few crimson lights, and parts of it were so tight she barely managed to squeeze through without ripping her dress. Blast it – of every colour under every sun, why had she chosen to wear *white*? She stood out in the darkness like a reactor core. An easy target.

Was it really that much colder in there, or was her mind playing tricks again?

A deafening blast roared through the silence, rattling the ship down to its metal bones. Leia gasped as she was thrown against a wall of circuits and pipes. The screams of blaster rifles and heavy marching steps thundered in her ears, muffling the screams and shouts of the men and women trying to hold off the invasion. They'd been boarded. And it sounded like the fight was raging right over her head.

Leia ran harder, until her lungs burned. *This is my fault,* she thought, tears stinging her eyes. *I told Father this was my mission. I just wanted him to be proud of me.* She had only wanted to help the Rebellion. Why did the crew have to lose their lives to save others?

Her father hadn't wanted her to accept the

mission; she had seen it on his face as he told her, "I don't doubt your capabilities, not even for a moment. Taking on all these responsibilities . . . they've shaped you into a glittering star. You are remarkable. But this is too dangerous, Leia."

Leia had fought to control her temper. A *star.* In other words, something beautiful. Something to be admired from a distance. The simpering princess her aunts had tried to force her to become her whole life. Someone who would ignore the calls of a rebellion desperate for help in stealing information.

She loved them with her whole heart, even when she felt like flipping the table over during her aunts' ruthless etiquette lessons and running away to join a galactic circus just so she wouldn't have to hear another lesson about the differences between a soup spoon and a dessert spoon. One day, yes, she would be queen of Alderaan like her mother before her, but that day was far off and there was more to being a fair ruler than learning the correct way to wave to her people. Her aunts had fought both Leia and her father on her joining the Galactic Senate. They would rather have seen her in her chambers twirling her hair and daydreaming about which snivelling prince to marry than in a Senate box trying to bring about real change and reform.

The press was even worse, claiming she was a "princess playing dress-up" and not a real diplomat and politician. They saw the image her aunts had crafted for her, not the person her father had trained her to become. No matter how many times she travelled the length of the galaxy to bring attention and aid to the suffering, still – *still* – the media refused to look past her label of "princess." One time she'd been holding an orphaned baby Wookiee, walking through a village the Imperial forces had burned to embers and ash, and the first question she'd taken from the reporters from the Central Systems was, who designed the outfit you're wearing?

Not, why are we here? Not, what can the galaxy do to help?

The only thing Leia had successfully managed

to do in her time in the Senate was irritate the Emperor like a sunburn that refused to fade. She'd gone into the chamber ready to fight anyone who stood in her way, and what she'd seen there had surprised her more than knocking heads with an opponent would have: no one seemed to care. Or at least no one wanted to test the Emperor's patience. She didn't understand how *anyone* could sit still in the Senate knowing about the crimes being committed in the Outer Rim.

Imperial interrogation camps. The execution of supposed traitors in cold blood. Whole cities destroyed in what Darth Vader called "purifications." Apparently, planets needed to be purified of any ideas resembling democracy. Or hope.

It made her sick. She could still smell the charred remains of buildings and lives. See the newly orphaned children lined up to be . . . what? Sold as labour to the highest bidder? Sent to the spice mines of Kessel? Every time Leia had tried to demand answers in the Senate chamber, she'd been reprimanded, silenced. She wanted to shout, shake them, force her colleagues to see what she saw. But they refused. Some told her to go back home, to enjoy palace life. Leia realised it didn't matter what she said, or how loudly she shouted. No one was listening.

So when Leia first learned of the Rebellion, she had all but jumped at the chance to be part of it – to be recognised for what she could do, not who she was. To actually *help* the galaxy. This was her chance to prove herself, and she thought her father would understand that, if nothing else.

Stealing top-secret plans from the Empire *was* a risk, but being dismissed as a twinkling ball of gas had only made her more determined. The mission should have been simple. All they needed to do was intercept a transmission about a new battle station the Empire was rumoured to be building.

But the system had been swarming with Imperials. They'd caught on to Leia's bogus tale about her ship's breaking down, but the cover had helped her stall long enough to download the technical plans for something code-named

"Death Star." Despite the Rebels' efforts to lose the Imperials in the jump to hyperspace, the hulking Star Destroyer had caught up to them. And Leia knew, the moment the ship identified itself as the *Devastator*, there would be no escape.

It was Darth Vader's ship.

She ran harder, ducking through shadows and bursts of warm steam. Her hand tightened around the data card as she made a sharp turn. Then something silver caught her eye.

A droid. An astromech droid, even. Thank the stars. Her plan actually had a chance of working.

The droid looked like an R2 unit. Its squat cylindrical body was topped with a dome-shaped head and panels of rich blue. A single indicator glowed red, then blue as the droid rolled by.

"Droid!" Leia called, tucking herself into a dark alcove. "Droid! Come here!"

The head swivelled towards her, letting out a friendly, questioning chirp. The droid rolled towards her on three legs, and Leia knelt down so she was level with it.

As much as she hated to admit it – and she hated it *a lot* – Leia was grateful her aunts had spent years drilling her on public speaking so that, as princess and someday queen, she could give speeches without embarrassing herself. She had to get the message right on the first try. There simply wasn't time to redo it. Leia closed her eyes a moment, steadying herself with deep breaths the way her aunts had shown her.

When she spoke, she was proud of how clear and careful the words were. "Artoo unit, I need to record the following holographic message. Do you have that programming, Artoo?"

The droid beeped in reply. Good enough.

Leia stood upright and stepped back. "Message begins . . . now." She cleared her throat, taking the regal tone her aunt loved, the one she'd sharpened like a knife in the Senate. "General Kenobi, years ago you served my father in the Clone Wars. Now he begs you to help him in his struggles against the Empire. I regret that I am unable to present my father's request to you in person, but my ship has fallen under attack and I'm afraid my mission to bring you to Alderaan has failed."

Admitting she failed made the words taste bitter in her mouth. Though she and the crew of the *Tantive IV* had downloaded the information and made the jump to Tatooine, she wouldn't be able to complete the second part of the mission. Her father had requested that she seek out an old friend, one General Kenobi, because, in his own words, "a war demanded warriors" to fight. A legendary Jedi Knight, Kenobi had gone into secret exile on the remote desert planet to avoid the deadly purge that had wiped out his order.

Leia pressed on. "I have placed information vital to the survival of the Rebellion into the memory system of this Artoo unit. My father will know how to retrieve it. You *must* see this droid safely to Alderaan. This is our most desperate hour. Help me, Obi-Wan Kenobi. You're my only hope."

Leia paused, wishing she felt more relieved than she did at having completed the message. But it was only the first step of one last, desperate mission, and she hated placing such valuable intelligence in the hands of a droid that didn't even possess hands.

"End of message. Now, here comes the truly difficult part, Artoo, I need you to deliver that message, along with the information I am about to upload to a man named Obi-Wan Kenobi. He resides on the planet beneath us, away from civilization. You'll need to search for him and him alone."

The droid rocked side to side on its back two legs, beeping in acknowledgment.

"Artoo? Artoo-Detoo! Where are you?"

Leia spun, looking for the source of the voice. She squinted, just barely making out the gold humanoid form of a protocol droid.

"Artoo!"

It was only then that Leia realised how quiet it had become. The firing and shouting had stopped, and some terrible part of her suspected it was because there was no one left from the *Tantive IV* to keep fighting. The crew's battle was over.

Hers was only beginning.

Leia's hands flew over the droid, inserting the data card. "Now you need a way off this ship . . . there should be at least one escape pod left for you to use. Do you follow?"

The R2 unit whistled another affirmative. Leia placed her hand on its smooth, round head and closed her eyes. *Please let this work. . . .*

"Good luck, safe travels."

The image of the planet below them floated to the front of her mind. Tatooine's endless sand dunes gave it a beautiful warm glow, like an eternal sunrise. She could see it now, as the droid rolled away, how he would struggle to navigate with the sand in his gears. But he could do it. She squeezed her hands into fists at her sides, pushing down the fear. Leia had faith.

"Artoo-Detoo, at last!" the protocol droid cried. "I've been looking all over for you!"

Leia drew her hood up over her head, carefully sliding her blaster out of its hidden holster. There was a way out for her; there had to be. Leia, like her father, refused to accept impossible odds. She just needed time to think. A safe place to hide. As the sounds and voices of the droids disappeared, new ones echoed over to her. Precise, sharp steps. The clicking of armour. Low voices.

Stormtroopers.

Leia pressed back farther into the shadows, squeezing her gun to keep her hand from shaking. She was all the droid had now. There was still time to create enough of a distraction for it to reach an escape pod and blast down to the planet's surface. But, stars, she couldn't get her heart to slow down. Her breathing sounded loud to her own ears. It wouldn't be her first time in a firefight – it wouldn't even be her first firefight that *month* – but there was so much at stake. She couldn't let all the lives lost that day be for nothing.

She *was* afraid. That the mission would be a failure. That the *Devastator* would blast the droid's escape pod into a trillion pieces. That she'd never return to Alderaan. That the Rebellion would be demolished. That she'd never see her father or mother again.

But fear was a useless emotion. She needed to fight, and the only way she knew how to burn through her fear was to summon her anger.

All she had to do was think of the Emperor's sickly eyes. His cackling laugh that crept all over her skin like freezing fingers.

Leia had met the evil old toad for the first time just after she'd been elected as Alderaan's senator. Her father was to present her to the Emperor on Coruscant, with all the newly elected officials. While her aunts had spent the days leading up to the trip debating her hairstyle and which dress she should wear, Leia had spent that time listing out her grievances. The things she'd be fighting to change. She wanted to tell the Emperor to his face. She was the youngest senator ever elected to the Imperial Senate, and she was going to make an impression – fire off a warning shot at the start of what was going to be a long war for the good of the galaxy. It didn't matter to her if she made some enemies in the process.

But as she had walked up to the black throne,

the old man had lifted his head, revealing the deathly pale, wrinkled skin of his face. His eyes had seemed to glow, piercing right through her. The words lodged in her throat, and a cold sweat broke out on her neck. Leia barely heard her father say her name, barely felt the hand he placed on her back to guide her forwards. Her aunts had drilled manners and protocol into her so deeply, she caught herself automatically dropping into a curtsy – a *curtsy*! – before she could stop herself.

"It will be nice," the Emperor croaked, a smirk twisting his bloodless lips, "to have such a pretty face in the Senate."

And that had been it. He had spoken to her like she was as much a piece of decoration as the chamber's statues. Leia hadn't been able to summon a single word to protest it. Just thinking about it made bile rise in her throat.

There. That was better. A steady, warm flush of anger flooded her system. Her focus sharpened, homing in on the stormtroopers stepping into the corridor through a nearby hatch.

"Search every passageway and compartment," the leader ordered. "You two, check behind those power conduits."

Of all the rotten luck – the pipe behind her released a hiss of steam and rattled loudly, making one of the stormtroopers turn back around.

"Wait. I thought I saw something – "

Blasted white dress, Leia thought, aiming her gun.

"There she is! Set your weapons to stun!"

Leia wasn't about to set *her* blaster to stun. She fired, hitting the stormtrooper out in front. He let out a sharp cry as he crashed to the ground.

"Watch it! She's armed! Fire!"

The firing would draw even more attention. She'd have to run, find better cover to hold them off just a little longer.

But the moment Leia turned her back, it felt like she'd been tackled from behind by a Star Destroyer. The hit from the stun bolt took all the feeling from her legs, sending her slamming forwards against the rough grating under her feet.

A thousand sparks of light burst in Leia's

eyes, momentarily blinding her.

Move! she ordered herself, even as helplessness rolled through her. *You're not done yet!*

"She'll be all right," she heard the first stormtrooper say. "Inform Lord Vader we have a prisoner."

CHAPTER TWO

SENSATION FLOODED back into Leia's numb arms and legs as she was hauled onto her feet. It felt like she'd been filled with sand. Her first few steps were stumbles, as the whole galaxy seemed to wobble around her. The stormtroopers surrounded her, snapping binders over her wrists.

They thought they could take her prisoner? *Her?* Leia knew she hadn't held much weight with the other senators, but she was well aware that the public cared about her. Any whisper of mistreatment would set the holonet on fire. Was that a risk the Emperor was willing to take?

She sincerely hoped not.

"H-how dare you!" she seethed, her lips still numb from the crackling electricity of the stun bolt. Even though it felt like her head was underwater, Leia twisted around, throwing her elbow back and kicking at the nearest stormtrooper's knee. In retaliation, the soldiers jostled her from all sides, shoving her forwards when she refused to move. Leia knew she was caught, but she wasn't going to be a willing captive.

The main corridor of the ship was almost blindingly bright after the dark interior passageways. Smoke from the battle choked the air. Every time Leia drew in a breath, her lungs burned with the sharp ozone stench left behind by blaster bolts.

And everywhere there were bodies.

They'd been left where they'd fallen, their wounds and lifeless expressions turning Leia's stomach violently. She didn't want to see that. Those were her people, and she'd marched them to their deaths. There was no way to fix that, no way to make it better. Leia forced herself to look, to remember. She'd need to tell their families . . . she'd need to . . . to . . .

My fault, she thought, *my fault . . .* Leia the senator, even Leia the princess, could justify their deaths as a necessary sacrifice, but Leia the human was having a hard time swallowing a scream.

Darth Vader stood at the end of the hallway, his towering height and wide shoulders almost blocking the hole the Imperials had blown through the doors to get into the *Tantive IV.* Stormtroopers swarmed around him, their armour clicking like the exoskeletons of insects. As the Emperor's right hand, Darth Vader stood out in sharp contrast. His armour, flowing cape and helmet were as black as the scorch marks on the walls.

And at his feet was the crumpled form of Captain Antilles. Leia could hear the loud wheeze of Vader's breathing as the stormtroopers dragged her forwards but couldn't detect any sign that the captain was alive.

Even him? Leia had been sure – or at least had hoped – they'd keep the captain alive for questioning. She'd banked on having his silent, steady support. Her chest seized with the shock of it, the pain. Her thoughts blanked out, overrun by anguish and fury.

Captain Antilles had been an extraordinary leader; he'd broken through countless Imperial blockades to get supplies to the Rebellion. And the crew had been so young, too – so much life wasted in a matter of minutes. She couldn't stand it. *The war will go on without me*, Captain Antilles had said. *It won't without you.* But in that moment, it all seemed impossible.

I'm sorry, she thought. *I'm so sorry.*

Civilian Leia was at a loss, but she felt some part of her click into place as she faced Darth Vader. Senator Leia Organa had dealt with him before. She could face him again. She could use the ice that flooded her veins to steel herself in his presence.

Leia straightened up, threw her shoulders back, hid her fear. But it was never easy to come face to face with a living nightmare. Especially when it towered over her. When its hot, moist breath fanned across her face as it leaned towards her.

"Darth Vader. I should have known." Leia

poured every ounce of the hate she felt into her voice. "Only you could be so bold. The Imperial Senate will not sit still for this. When they hear you've attacked a diplomatic – "

"Don't play games with me, Your Highness. You weren't on any mercy mission this time. You passed directly through a restricted system!" Not for the first time, Leia thought he must have intentionally programmed his voice to be deep and rumbling, like a thunderstorm. No normal man could sound half as terrifying. "Several transmissions were beamed to this ship by Rebel spies. I want to know what happened to the plans they sent you."

Leia tried to ignore the way her heart was galloping in her chest. The little droid would have to be away by now, shooting down to the planet, out of Vader's reach. She had outmanoeuvred him, maybe for the first time ever, and knowing that made it easier to keep her cool. "I don't know what you're talking about. I'm a member of the Imperial Senate on a diplomatic mission."

"You're part of the Rebel Alliance and a traitor!"

he roared, swinging around to a nearby storm-trooper. "Take her away!"

At his command, the stormtroopers pushed her towards the hole they'd blown though the door of the *Tantive IV*. Leia strained her ears, trying to catch what an Imperial officer was reporting to Vader. She caught only a few words: *We must be careful. . . . The people adore her. . . . Rebels . . . princess . . . plans . . .*

Blast it – Vader knew exactly what information they'd downloaded. The Rebellion and all its members – including her father – were in more danger than ever, and it tore at her heart to know that it was her fault for letting the ship, the crew, and herself fall into the Empire's net. As Leia left her battered ship for what she knew would be the last time, she could only hope she'd given that little droid enough of a chance to save them all.

CHAPTER THREE

———————— ✦ ————————

ONE OF THE MANY dangers of being born
royal – aside from death by boredom during
her aunts' lessons – was the constant threat
of abduction. As her mother was the queen
of Alderaan and her father the queen's consort,
to say they were wealthy and powerful was a vast
understatement. When the seediest cretins came
crawling out of the darkest corners of the galaxy
looking for victims, Leia was a natural target for
their greed. So despite feeling there was something terribly unladylike about throwing large,
sweaty men around on wrestling mats, her aunts
agreed with her parents that self-defense needed
to become part of her relentless princess training
once she turned sixteen.

Leia had loved the rush that feeling physically

strong had given her; it was the same buzzing sensation she felt every time she did something useful for the Rebellion. Plus, the self-defense lessons had their unexpected uses. For instance, being able to punch a dummy made it easier to turn around later in the afternoon and learn ten different ways to curtsy without kicking her aunts in the shins. And a single piece of advice from her instructor had saved her life a hundred times over: *pay attention*.

Leia kept her mind clear and focused on the moment, her eyes open and scanning the Star Destroyer and every Imperial soldier around her. They had brought the *Tantive IV* into a hangar bay that was mostly deserted – of course. Leia was still a member of the Senate, and Vader would do everything in his vast power to hush up this incident. Including, if she had to guess, destroying her ship and blaming her "unfortunate death" on some kind of mechanical malfunction.

Her stomach clenched, twisted into knots. No, they hadn't killed her on the spot, but Leia was certain it had nothing to do with her being a senator or a princess and everything to do with the answers Vader thought he could get out of her.

What would happen after he realised she'd give him nothing about the Rebellion? Leia would willingly jump out of an airlock into the freezing vacuum of space before she would betray her father and the people she'd come to think of as comrades.

She had to get out – get the *truth* out. If she could just get down to Tatooine and find the droid and General Kenobi, she could still salvage the mission. And, if nothing else, she could tell her father she was still alive. Leia burned with the need to prove she hadn't failed him or the Rebellion completely. She would never let herself wallow in the helplessness the Senate had tried to drown her in. There was still too much to do.

The Star Destroyer's interior was exactly like the regime it served: cold and ruthlessly efficient. It was all sleek lines, everything in pure white or black. There was no grey in the Emperor's world.

There was *us* and there was *them*. There was *his way* or *no way* at all.

Leia was hustled into a narrow silver tube of an elevator that shot her and her escorts up to a walkway at breakneck speed. She leaned around the broad shoulders and shining armour of the stormtroopers, trying to dodge their grips to see what was below. A series of hangars, as it turned out. Each wide, echoing chamber featured impossibly tall ceilings and enormous metal doors to draw ships inside.

You could fit the entire population of some planets in here, Leia thought, shocked at their size. She saw sparks spraying up as engineers worked to repair ships, droids hauling in heavy pieces of machinery no man could have ever lifted, and assembled lines of troops drilling in formations.

Compared with the others, the hangar they'd towed the *Tantive IV* into was smaller, but already swarming with stormtroopers and Imperial officers. It was the third hangar they passed that caught and held Leia's attention. There were two shuttles docked below, with only a single crew moving carts of supplies towards them.

Someone's prepping for a trip, she thought. Her mind worked at lightspeed, and she saw her escape plan unfold as clearly as if the Emperor himself had rolled out a carpet for her. *Yes* – a small thrill of victory raced through her. She could work with that. Her spirits lightened for the first time in hours, and she felt the crushing pressure lift off her chest. The shuttles would be fueled. And the shuttles were outfitted with weapons. She could blast her way out, and by the time they realised what was happening, she'd be through Tatooine's atmosphere.

Take that! she wanted to shout to the other senators. She was about to prove exactly what she was capable of when given the opportunity to *try*. Her membership in the Rebellion still felt new, too fresh. She'd needed the mission to show them her dedication and how far she'd go for them if only they'd give her the support to get there. This – the story of her escape under Vader's nose – would solidify her bond with them that much more. No one – not the media, not her aunts, not even her father – would be able to deny that she was a fighter and deserved to have her voice heard.

If I don't get shot out of the sky first, she thought. No – she could do it. She'd had years of flight training. And, well, there were all those dunes to hide in. Let's see how Vader liked getting gritty sand in sensitive places in his armour.

She found her chance as two of her escorts broke away, heading into a nearby command room – if she had to guess, to begin processing her into the detention block. Leia allowed the others to push her into yet another elevator. The doors had barely shut when she swung her bound hands towards the control panel with a *thwack*, causing the car to jerk to a stop. The stormtroopers next to her were thrown off balance, giving her the chance to swipe one of their blasters and fire.

"Stop – !"

Too late for that, laser brain, Leia thought, glancing down at their stunned forms. Neither of them had the key to her binders. She reached up to pull one of the dozens of pins out of her hair and went to work jamming the electronic lock. Like the binders mattered. She could fly herself out of there blind, deaf and with both arms and legs bound behind her back.

The second the elevator door hissed open, Leia slipped out and scanned the empty hall. She turned back and fired a shot at the elevator's control panel. The doors shrieked in protest, jamming over and over on one of the stormtroopers' feet. Leia blew a stray piece of hair out of her eyes in a huff of annoyance as she kicked the foot back into the car. The elevator door slammed shut.

Leia kept to the edge of the corridor, hanging back a few steps from the hangar's entrance. The air on the ship was dry and freezing cold, but Leia felt damp with sweat. Pulse fluttering, she watched the engineers step through the hangar door together, speaking quietly. They turned, heading away from her.

Leia was still clutching the stolen blaster as

she slipped inside and made a run for the shuttle. The boarding ramp was down – her mind sorted through the dangers quickly, like she was flicking through a stack of sabacc cards.

If no one was on board, she could just *go*.

If someone was on board, she'd need to stun him, but she could use him as a hostage. Stars, her aunts would have expired on the spot hearing *that* un-princess-like thought.

Two or three people inside would pose somewhat more of a challenge – the thought slid to a halt at the same moment her feet did.

Standing at the top of the shuttle's boarding ramp, hands on his hips, as solid and large as any of Alderaan's mountains, was Darth Vader.

CHAPTER FOUR

FOR A MOMENT, Leia's breath caught in her throat.

"An admirable show of spirit," Vader's voice boomed. There was a hint of amusement in it that somehow made her anger flame hotter than her irritation at having been caught. Leia set her jaw to keep from grinding her teeth. He was mocking her! "But the innocent have no reason to flee."

Blast it, she thought. She should have known he'd only use her escape attempt as more proof against her. Time to pull out the one weapon she had and hope she aimed true. "I am a member of the Imperial Senate. I have rights, including the right not to be illegally detained!"

"You wear that title like armour, thinking it will protect you. No more, *Your Highness*. You have no rights and no protection now. The Imperial Senate is being dealt with as we speak."

He stalked down the ramp, his heavy footsteps thundering in her ears. For a moment, Leia didn't understand. "Dealt with" – did that mean – ?

"Yes," Vader said, circling around her. The blaster flew out of her hands, sailing through the air to land in his. She whirled around, stunned. The now-familiar cold prickle she associated with him was back, drawing freezing fingers up and down her neck.

When Leia was young, and fairly shameless about eavesdropping on her parents' conversations, she'd overheard her father speaking about how Vader instilled fear in everyone around him – how he could control not only people but objects. Her father called it the Force. What she knew of this mystic energy and its power she knew from hearing stories of the Jedi, the knights who defended the Old Republic. But, unless she'd misunderstood her father's tales, the Jedi had been good, kind, dedicated to peace. How could someone as twisted and heartless as Vader have mastered their power?

Leia was so caught up in her thoughts, she nearly missed the verbal blow he delivered next.

"The Emperor has disbanded the Senate. You are no longer a senator. What defense will you use now, I wonder?"

The hollow feeling at the centre of Leia's chest billowed out, shriveling up even the unkind comparison she was about to make between Vader and a protocol droid missing crucial parts of its verbobrain.

You are no longer a senator.

Leia hadn't served long on the Senate, but she'd spent *years* fighting to be trained for the role. She'd let herself shape her future around that dream, the way it would open up her world beyond the quiet, dull, strangely powerless existence of being a princess. The disappointment of realizing no one in the Senate would ever see her as anything more had soured her feelings towards the idea, but she hadn't let it go. The Rebellion was her way to see out her goals for a more peaceful, prosperous galaxy, but the Senate was supposed to be there at the end to help rebuild the galaxy once the Emperor was gone.

Apparently, the Empire was still capable of surprising her with its cruelty, its complete disregard for the law. Never for a moment did she consider that the Senate might cease to exist.

In an instant her dreams had collapsed in on themselves like a black hole forming. And Leia felt . . . hollow.

Vader strode past her, towards the hangar's entrance. "You will follow me, or I will make you follow me. Your choice."

I need time, she thought, the blood pounding in her ears, *time to figure out another way.* And she knew enough to understand that the best way to find that time and, more important, stay alive was to play the part of the prisoner.

So Leia decided, wisely, not to tempt him, seeing as he could probably lift her using only his little finger – or, she supposed, the Force. Her nostrils flared in frustration at the thought of being yanked around the way her blaster had been. His black cape swept out behind him, tempting her to slam a foot down on it just to see if he was capable of tripping.

Darth Vader's appearance on the dark control deck sent the officers scattering back to their stations. Leia had never seen so many backs go rigid at once, like he'd yanked them all up by the hair.

She turned towards the viewport, surprised to see the stars streaking by. When had they jumped to hyperspace?

An older man in a neat grey uniform quickly made his way over to them. Leia recognised him as a captain by the arrangement of coloured squares attached to his chest. That and the way his voice shook. She'd heard Vader had a way of "disposing" of the officers who disappointed him, which seemed to be everyone he crossed paths with. Judging by the way the man looked – like he'd blissfully lick Vader's boots clean if asked – Leia didn't doubt it.

"Status, Captain?"

"We're right on schedule, Lord Vader. Coming out of hyperspace shortly."

Shortly was a few moments later. Leia stood at Vader's side, hands bound again in a way that was making her feel capable of committing some very Vader-like behaviour. The officers on the deck stared at her openly, whispering to one another.

"Where are you taking me?" she demanded. "I still have diplomatic immunity as a princess of Alderaan."

"We've already arrived at our destination."

Leia spun back towards the viewport. She was still, after everything, expecting to see Coruscant, the capitol planet. But there was only a small grey moon hovering in the sea of stars.

A moon that wasn't orbiting a planet? No, it had to be a small planet. It grew larger . . . larger . . . *larger* as they moved towards it, until it filled the viewport completely.

Leia's heart sank to her feet.

That wasn't . . .

It couldn't be . . .

How . . . ?

The stars weren't winking around the hulking sphere as she'd first thought. The flickering lights were swarms of TIE fighters moving in formation, screeching as they passed the approaching *Devastator*. Those weren't craters marring the sphere's surface, but plating and towers. The large crater she'd spotted right away was no crater at all – it almost looked like a circular dish.

Leia realised she was trembling and clenched her hands tightly to hide it.

"Death Star . . ." The words came out in a horrified whisper.

A second too late, Leia realised her grave mistake.

Vader turned on his heel. "Yes, the Death Star. The *secret* weapon you claim to know nothing about. The plans you claim you do not possess. Really, Your Highness, you made that far too easy."

Blast. She could blame it on exhaustion or fear, but Leia might as well have just dangled the data card in his face. *Think, think, think.* She fumbled for a reasonable explanation, her pulse pounding in her ears. "No, there were whispers of it in the Senate – "

Vader talked right over her. "Look closely. Do you see the dish? That is the prime weapon. When it fires, the galaxy will finally understand the Empire's might."

And the Rebellion could be virtually wiped out in a single shot.

"You're mad. This is *insane!*"

"No, Your Highness," he said, "this is power."

"Then why worry about your missing plans?" she shot back. "If you're so powerful, if the station is invincible, why does it matter – ?"

He sliced a hand through the air, cutting her off again. "Since you are so curious about our new battle station, you'll be pleased to know you'll be our first honoured guest. Your quarters are being prepared for your arrival. Should you choose to continue to be uncooperative, you will find your stay immediately shortened. Permanently. Do you understand?"

Leia gritted her teeth but nodded.

"Know that there will be no escape this time, Princess," he warned. "To try would be . . . foolish."

Sometimes, she thought, just sometimes, it was good to be underestimated. Leia turned back to the viewport, taking in the looming battle station with new eyes. Vader and his lackeys would find that out soon enough.

CHAPTER FIVE

AS SHE WAS TRANSFERRED to the Death Star by shuttle, Leia kept her eyes open. Wide open.

She mentally mapped out the path they took from the hangar to a set of elevators, counted each turn and the steps down every hall. She counted the clusters of marching stormtroopers as they made their way down the glossy corridors, noting which direction they marched. Droids zipped around her feet, and, blast it, she was thinking of the other droid again, the little R2 rolling through the desert sand dunes. Leia knew she needed to keep her mind clear and free of every guilty thought – which, unfortunately, became more and more of a challenge with each mistake she made.

There was no doubt in her mind about what was coming next.

Vader had assigned eight stormtroopers to her detail. A part of her was proud. But, mostly, she just wanted to roll her eyes, especially when they all tried to cram into the elevator together.

She was brought up to the detention block without a word of explanation. Stepping through the last door, they were met with the faces of three startled security officers as they looked up from their consoles. Leia took some satisfaction in the fact that their eyes bugged out a little. They recognised her. Good. That meant she'd been doing her job as the official needlebug in the Emperor's side.

"This is prisoner two-one-eight-seven," one of her escorts said.

The security officer shook his head, confused. "But that's Senator – "

"*This is prisoner two-one-eight-seven*," the stormtrooper repeated.

Of course. In Vader's eyes, she was no longer

a senator. She wasn't a princess, either. She was a low enough life form that she no longer deserved a name. She was a criminal. This was going to be . . . a tricky situation. If she couldn't convince them that she wasn't involved with the Rebellion, she'd be marked as a criminal and would likely never be able to return home to Alderaan. Not until the Rebellion had overthrown the Empire, at least. And while Leia was growing more excited at the prospect of joining the Rebel Alliance fully – living, fighting, working with them every day – she couldn't wrap her head around the fact that it might be years before she saw her parents again.

The security officer stared at the stormtrooper. The stormtrooper stared at the security officer.

"After hours of being mistreated and manhandled," Leia said, doing her best impression of her aunts, "I've grown rather bored with the incompetence around me and would like to be shown to my quarters. Unless doing your jobs is asking too much?"

She knew full well that her quarters were a prison cell, but she'd jump out of an air lock before acknowledging that fact.

"Er – very well," the security officer said.

Leia was pushed forwards again, and she stepped up and around the raised control consoles. She scanned the badly lit stretch of hall in front of her, shivering at the freezing touch of the oxygen hissing up through the vents in the floor. From what she could see, there was only one entrance to the detention block, and that was the one she had come through. Cell door, cell door, cell door, a hatch for a garbage chute – the stormtrooper in front of her stopped so abruptly that Leia crashed into his back.

They at least removed her binders before shoving her inside. Leia stumbled into the long, flat sheet of metal on the opposite side of the cramped room. Her bed, if she had to guess. Whirling around, she came within a few centimetres of kicking the closed door before stopping herself.

"You won't get away with this!" she called. "Do you hear me?"

Leia was ready to tear the station apart, even if she had to do it with her bare hands.

But first she had to get herself out of that cell.

Leia paced in circles, feeling at the seams of the walls for loose panels that could be pried off, if not to reveal a hidden escape route, then to be used as weapons. Everything on the space station was new and pristine. Turning her attention upward, she climbed onto the metal cot and scanned the ceiling – there! The red light pouring through the grates covering the ceiling had masked it at first, but there it was. A vent.

A vent the size of her head.

Her excitement flared out. Leia half sat, half collapsed back down onto the cot, blowing out a frustrated sigh. For that particular escape route to work, she'd need to be as small as a Kowakian monkey-lizard to fit through the opening and as tall as a Wookiee to reach it.

Hungry, tired, cold and now extremely put out,

she swung her legs up and hugged them to her chest. From palace to prison. She could see the holonet headlines now.

Darth Vader didn't keep her waiting long. Leia supposed the opportunity to watch her squirm was too much for him to resist. She was, however, surprised that he was willing to do the dirty work himself.

The door hissed open and his dark shape swept in, followed closely by two security officers. The two men fell into place on either side of the door, their gazes fixed on the ceiling. For a long, terrible second, there was no sound in the small cell beyond the steady wheeze of Vader's respirator. A cold drip of alarm ran down Leia's back.

"I hope you find your quarters adequate, Princess."

Leia raised her chin. No fear. No breaking. No screaming. *Prove it to yourself,* she thought. *Prove that you deserve to be one of them.*

This was for her father and the Rebellion he

had helped establish, the one she would continue to help build.

"I demand to be released and given a formal trial," she said.

"Spare me your indignation," Vader said. "I've neither the time nor the patience for it."

A strange sound – a beeping that sizzled through the air like a bolt of static – made the hair rise on Leia's neck. Vader stepped aside, allowing a spherical droid to float in behind him. It bobbed slightly as it came towards her, its glossy black exterior shot through with silver and punctuated by a red eye light.

"What – ?" she began, pressing back against the wall of her cell.

Gleaming silver blades and rods rose out of the droid's shell, but Leia's eyes were focused on the syringe that emerged from its side and began filling with some kind of liquid. A wicked-looking needle, long as her hand, was aimed directly at her.

"No!" she shouted. Leia knew what that was – an interrogation droid. They were illegal, considered too inhumane for use. Stars, she was an idiot. Nothing was too inhumane for the Empire.

"This is your last chance, Your Highness," Vader warned. "If you will not tell me where the plans are and where I'll find the Rebels' fortress, I will *force* the answers from you."

Leia's breath came in rapid bursts. Holding out against interrogation had been part of her self-defense training, but this – this was so much worse than anything she could have imagined. Pain and humiliation could be pushed away, boxed up inside, but a truth serum?

There was nowhere to run. Leia bolted towards the door, but Vader's arms locked around her, swinging her back into the interrogation droid's path. The pain that lanced through her arm as the needle punctured her skin and the serum seeped into her system was unbearable.

She collapsed back against the wall, shaking her head. It felt light enough to float away. Her vision blurred at the edges, making her feel as if she were walking through an early morning fog on the palace grounds, the soft sunlight warming her skin – but no, *no*, that wasn't right. Leia wasn't on Alderaan.

A voice floated to her through the clouds. "Your Highness, you're safe. You can trust me."

Leia shook her head, turning her face against something cold, hard, smooth. *Cell.* She was in a cell. On the – on the – Why couldn't she hold on to a thought? Her pulse was pounding in her ears again. She pressed her hands against them. Not safe. Not safe. Not safe.

Death Star . . . the words floated up to the front of her mind. That's where she was. Not on Alderaan. The thought made pain streak through her. Made her dizzy. Why wouldn't it stop? Where was her father? She wanted her father – "I'm with the Rebel Alliance," the voice continued. "I need to know what you did with the Death Star plans. You *must* tell me. You *must* trust me."

There was a bad taste in her mouth, a pounding in her skull. Leia was so sure she was going to be sick, she bent at the waist, ignoring the way fire seemed to stream through her blood. Words popped like bubbles in her mind.

Interrogation.

Death.

Star.

Vader.

"We need them, Leia! Tell me where to find the plans!"

"L-leave me alone." *Interrogation. Rebels. Can't tell the truth. Don't tell the truth. Antilles.* Tantive IV. *Alderaan. Senate. Galaxy.*

Slowly, as if stretching after a long sleep, her mind started to sharpen. Leia remembered where she was, even with her head feeling light enough to float away, her lips loose enough to spill every secret she protected. *Trained.* She'd been trained.

You'll be forced to give information, her instructor had said, *truthful information. But it doesn't have to be* current *information. There's always a way to give a truth that's related but not the answer they want. Find a connection.*

"*Where are the plans?*" The voice exploded in her ears, loud enough to make Leia cringe.

"I don't have them!" she shouted. "I don't have them!"

"*Where* are they?"

"I don't have them!" she repeated.

"Where did you send them? Where is the Rebel base?"

Without warning, the fire in Leia's body was blown out, replaced by an icy grip. Fear wound its way through her, snaking down into her stomach. The feeling was so different from the light-headed dream of the serum. There was . . . *power* behind each of his words. They nudged at her. They prodded as sharply as any knife. So Leia did the only thing she could – she pulled back. Physically, towards the wall. Mentally, to a place the voice couldn't find her. An unfamiliar warmth wrapped around her, a protective blanket that didn't let any of the darkness nudge through.

The freezing pressure on her mind was thrown back. The rumbling voice made a sound of surprise and was quiet for a long moment. "If you do not tell me where to find the Rebels, lives will be lost! All of the Rebel deaths will be on your head!"

"Leave me alone!" Leia repeated, throwing her arms up over her head.

"Your father wants you to trust us," the voice said, softer now. "He wants you to tell us where to find the Rebels. He's worried about you. He wants you to come home."

"Alderaan is my home." That was true.

"Are you a member of the Rebel Alliance?"

Leia swallowed the disgusting taste in the back of her mouth, blinking as the cell began to take shape again around her. Vader was a black blur against the crimson ceiling lights. *Not safe.*

"I'm Princess Leia Organa," she said. "I'm the senator from Alderaan."

And that was the truth.

Vader stepped back, watching her as stilly and silently as any poisonous snake about to strike. He began to turn, signalling something to the security officers. Leia slumped back against the metal cot in relief. They were leaving. It was over.

"Careful," Vader warned. "If you continue to resist, soon you will be neither."

The cell door hissed shut behind him.

CHAPTER SIX

WITH NO CLOCK ON THE WALL, it was easy to lose track of time.

Despite her best efforts to stay awake, exhaustion finally wrestled her into a troubled sleep. She felt herself drift in and out of consciousness each time boots echoed down the hallway outside. The truth serum had finally left her system, which meant her stomach had stopped clenching and flipping each time she took a breath.

I did it, she thought, letting pride and a small happiness warm the ice that still gripped her centre. She hadn't broken under any amount of agony. There was that, at least – even her aunts would have been impressed she'd managed to keep her head in such a dangerous situation. But it was a cold comfort. She was alone with the small, shivering fear that Vader could come back any second with that droid, and that next time he would try something else. And that he would finally yank the truth out of her.

Had minutes passed? Hours? A day?

I can do it again, she told herself. *I can make it.*

She knew that as long as she stayed in her cell, her life would be nothing more than a ticking clock. There wasn't a single doubt in her mind that her father was searching for clues about what happened to her, but she couldn't sit on her hands and hope he or someone in the Rebellion would put everything together. Leia had to rescue herself.

The truth was Leia couldn't predict how long Vader would keep her alive knowing there was a chance she was connected to the Rebellion. It seemed out of character for him to give her even this much time to come around – unusually patient for someone who didn't blink at crushing a subordinate like a worm.

If he was even capable of blinking . . . What was under that mask, exactly?

Leia pushed herself up, rubbing the sleep from her eyes. She was on a space station. There had to be *some* way for her to get a message to Alderaan. An officer would be too concerned with his or her next promotion to risk sympathising with Leia, but she'd seen the surprised faces of the security officers when she'd come in. Was it possible that there were soldiers within the Empire who didn't agree with their master's policies? Leia knew that service in the military wasn't always voluntary. . . .

The heavy steps outside her cell door interrupted the new plan forming in her mind. For a moment, Leia was convinced that she could feel the ground shake – but maybe that was just her own fright playing tricks on her. No more than a moment later, she heard the familiar *click* and *whoosh* of Vader's respirator. Then the door opened.

Leia jumped to her feet, but neither Darth Vader nor the two security officers with him actually stepped inside.

"Follow me." Vader's cloak flew out behind him as he turned.

Equal parts curious and nervous, Leia took a tentative step outside of her cell. Were they transporting her again? Taking her to some kind of trial? Or was this the moment they'd get rid of her once and for all?

The security officer snapped binders over her wrists, tight enough to make Leia cringe. Without a word of explanation, they led her through the detention block, boots clicking on the metal walkway in time with the throbbing headache behind her eyes. The burn of the outer hallway's bright lights was unbearable. Everything on the ship was shining and new, gleaming with evil intentions.

Vader caught her by the shoulder as they approached two towering metal doors. They slid open at his signal, a whisper of a sound that faded into silence.

That was what struck Leia first: the quiet. There were dozens of men and women in black uniforms and helmets seated along a stretch of control panels that held too many glowing buttons and levers even to attempt to count. Over their heads, more panels blinked with red and white lights.

It was the control room, Leia realised, the over-bridge. They had walked her into the nerve centre of the Death Star.

But . . . why would they show her this?

At the opposite end of the chamber, an enormous screen blinked to life, illuminating the officer standing in front of it.

Of course. Of course it would be *him*.

"Governor Tarkin," Leia began with her sweetest face. "I should have expected to find you holding Vader's leash. I recognised your foul stench when I was brought on board."

The very first thing Leia's father had ever told her about Grand Moff Wilhuff Tarkin was that she was to stay away from him. He had made an official visit to Alderaan right around the time Leia had turned thirteen – which, coincidentally, was also about the time when Leia had made it her mission to do the opposite of whatever she was told to do.

So she'd crept along the halls of the palace behind the two men, listening to the cold, tense words they exchanged.

As she'd slipped out of her hiding place, one thought had blasted through her mind: *he is a snake.* A man who kept slaves. A man who wrapped around his victims and slowly, mercilessly crushed the life from them.

The cold, sharp edges of his heart were reflected in the lines of his face. As the years had gone on and he'd aged into his ugly cruelty, his skin had pulled tight against his skull. His steely blue eyes could assess a person's worth in a single glance, and the perpetually sour expression on his face showed that he always found the person lacking.

Behind him, a beautiful emerald-green planet filled the screen, glowing with life. Leia felt her chest clench at the sight of it. That was Alderaan. They must have travelled there after bringing her aboard.

That was her home – the sight she'd been longing to see from the moment she'd left it. Despite everything, she was floating on a bubble of excitement. Were they really releasing her, then?

"Charming to the last," Tarkin said, with a look that would have caused a freshly bloomed rose to wither. "You don't know how hard I found it signing the order to terminate your life."

Apparently not.

A jolt of fear shot through her. Leia had expected they might kill her, of course, but it was one thing to think it and another to hear it promised so casually, the way someone would announce what was for supper.

"I'm surprised you had the courage to take the responsibility yourself," she shot back.

There. His eye gave a small twitch. Leia tilted her head to the side, her lips twisted into a smirk. Very few things made her happier than getting a rise out of despicable old men who wanted everyone around them to cower in their presence.

These men *wanted* her to beg for her life. To tremble and cry. It was time to let her hatred fly, to show them once and for all she was not that girl. She was *not* that little princess. "However did you choose the method of my demise without the Emperor there to pat you on the head when you finished?"

The governor clasped his hands together in front of him, angling his face back towards the screen. Another officer stepped up beside him, struggling to master his smirk at her words. He was younger than Tarkin, his face stirring some memory at the back of Leia's mind. Admiral . . . Motti. Wonderful. No wonder the Death Star was so big – it needed to be to house some of the largest egos in the galaxy.

"Princess Leia, before your execution, I would like you to be my guest at a ceremony that will make this battle station operational." He was so smug, so sure of himself. There wasn't a single aspect of Tarkin that didn't make Leia's skin want to crawl right off her bones. "No star system will dare oppose the Emperor now."

"The more you tighten your grip," Leia warned, "the more star systems will slip through your fingers."

"Not after we demonstrate the power of this station." The little smirk he gave her made Leia want to take a small step back. A man like him didn't smile unless he was about to get a taste of blood. "In a way, you have determined the choice of the planet that'll be destroyed first. Since you are reluctant to provide us with the location of the Rebel base, I have chosen to test this station's destructive power . . . on your home planet of Alderaan."

The truth whipped through her, cracking her wide open with terror. "No! Alderaan is peaceful. We have no weapons. You can't possibly . . ."

They couldn't. Alderaan was one of the central planets. The galaxy depended on its wealth and innovation. There were billions of innocent lives down there!

"You would prefer another target? A military target? Then name the system!" Tarkin said. "Where is the Rebel base?"

Leia glanced over at the officers sitting at the controls of the station, disbelief swelling inside her. How could they follow orders like these? She pulled back, trying to hide her face so they wouldn't see that panic had drained every last drop of blood from it. But Vader was like a wall behind her, and Tarkin stepped up close in front of her, trying to get her to cower.

A version of the truth, she thought, *old information.* The location would be believable, and she wouldn't run the risk of giving them a planet they had already checked and found clear of Rebel activity. It didn't matter that she'd be confirming her involvement with the Rebellion once and for all, not if it meant saving her planet. She would have fought through years of war to help the Rebellion, but she would die for her home.

"Dantooine," Leia said softly, lowering her head. "They're on Dantooine."

"There. You see, Lord Vader, she can be reasonable." Tarkin turned towards Admiral Motti. "Continue with the operation. You may fire when ready."

"What?" Leia cried. "I gave you what you wanted! You can't do this!"

"You're far too trusting," Tarkin said, giving a dismissive wave. "Dantooine is too remote to make an effective demonstration. But don't worry. We will deal with your Rebel friends soon enough."

"No!" Leia begged. "Please!"

"Commence primary ignition," one of the officers said, leaning forwards over his section of the console to push one of a dozen lit buttons on the panel. Next to him, another officer reached up to pull a lever.

The low, eerie hum vibrated through the floor, through Leia's skin. She felt it in her teeth. Vader's grip on her tightened as a green beam appeared in the viewport. Leia sucked in a horrified gasp, struggling against him, trying to do something – anything – to – The beam of light raced towards her planet, ripping through the blackness of space. There was a single moment when everything around Leia seemed to suspend. She didn't breathe. Didn't move. Couldn't feel. And then – The planet gleaming like a gemstone in front of her exploded, tearing apart in a burst of fiery light, sending debris scattering into a molten hot ring. She could imagine how it happened. How the light must have appeared in the crystal blue sky for just a moment. How the mountains had dissolved into dust. Billions of lives gone in the blink of an eye.

Her home. Her *family*.

She stood there, seconds feeling like hours. She shook her head again. There was no way. Alderaan couldn't be gone. It was all a show, some strange illusion that the Empire had crafted to try to break her. Another interrogation tactic.

But then why would they have done it after she had given them the information they were looking for? Why were the fragments of the planet's core still shooting out around them, blazing paths across the void of space.

It was real.

The cold numbness that had gripped her suddenly snapped. In its place was a burning, bottomless anger.

Leia screamed, trying to rip herself out of Vader's grip to claw at Tarkin's face with every ounce of fury radiating from her centre. Vader held her firmly, letting her struggle against his iron grip.

"You call yourselves human?" she snarled.

Tarkin merely gave her a bored look, then turned to Vader. "Take her back to her cell to await termination. Sedate her if you must."

There was no need. Her shocked rage flared so bright, so hot that it burned out before she could really make use of it. And once it was gone, she was left with nothing but numb disbelief. Her home . . . her family . . . everything . . . It didn't feel real, any of it. Her mother, her father, her aunts, her people, the gardens, her room, the libraries, the art, the beautiful blooming life – the Empire needed to take her instead. She would do anything to bring it all back. She would trade herself, *anything*, if they could undo what they'd done.

You know that's impossible, a small voice whispered in her mind. Nothing would bring her home back. No amount of bargaining would fix this. It was over.

They must have dragged her back to her cell. Leia didn't remember. Her legs gave out the moment she was through the cell door. The next thing she knew, her cheek was pressed against the cold metal grating on the floor. Her fingers curled around it, but Princess Leia Organa of Alderaan, for the first time in her life, couldn't bring herself to push herself back onto her feet.

Princess Leia. Were you still a princess if your home world was gone?

In a matter of hours, she'd lost her position in the Senate, her home, and every plan she'd made. For the first time in her life, Leia didn't know what to do. The senator didn't have a plan. The princess didn't have a history. All that was left was just . . . Leia.

She closed her eyes, trying to picture her parents' faces. Her body shook with the effort to keep her tears back. She folded the pain away, the anguish. She had to. She'd made a promise to her father as he'd seen her and the crew of the *Tantive IV* off that last time: *I won't fail you.* But hadn't she?

No. *No.* Leia pushed her chest off the ground, sitting up. Failing would be giving up. Because somewhere out in the desert there was a droid carrying the hope for the future inside of him. There were allies counting on her, allies who needed to know the truth about the Death Star and the tremendous danger they were in. It wouldn't be the same, but she could still fight. She had a place with the Rebel Alliance.

Leia took a deep breath, her father's voice whispering in her mind. *Taking on all of these responsibilities . . . they've shaped you into a glittering star.*

Maybe she had misunderstood what he meant after all. Her father hadn't been a man who prided himself on his riches or owning beautiful things. He didn't value gems or credits, and he didn't often fall back on poetic flattery. Above all, he admired strength. And how else were stars formed but through a collision of pressure and heat, an explosion of energy? The formation of a star shaped the space around it. It could be seen from millions of kilometres away.

She stood up, straightening to her full height, and began to look around her cell again, searching for her out. They could think they'd taken the parts of her that mattered most. That they'd broken her. But there was a part of Leia that the Emperor, Vader, Tarkin, any of them could never touch.

Her heart was a star that would never burn out.

And she would outshine them all.

THE
SCOUNDREL

NOTHING LIKE A severed limb flying through the air to break up a perfectly good day in a cantina.

"No blasters!" the barkeep called, panicked. "No blasters!"

Thank the stars, Han thought. Otherwise no one would walk out of there alive.

For a single heartbeat, the thick herbal smoke that layered the air seemed to part. The band's cheerful music cut out. The shouts in Basic and what had to be every other language in the galaxy faded to a whimper. For the first time in Chalmun's Cantina's long history of hosting the rowdiest pirates Mos Eisley had to offer, there was absolute silence.

Then everyone went back to their business and

the pulse of life returned. The band, Figrin D'an and the Modal Nodes, a group of Bith with dome-shaped heads and black, glassy insect eyes, started bopping away on their instruments again.

Han could have sworn the severed arm – not to mention the creature's remaining stump – was still sizzling when the old fossil calmly switched his blue laser sword off. Han leaned around the girl in his lap, trying to see what had sparked the fight in the first place. A younger human, a blonde teenager, was hauled up from the floor looking dazed, then disappeared into one of the cantina's dark pockets.

Han had taken up a corner booth back in the shadows, waiting for the right job to lure him out. And, well, OK, it had the added bonus of keeping him out of sight of the people hunting his skin. But clearly Han should have been more worried about the human girl training her sights on him than he was about Jabba the Hutt.

"Han . . ." the girl in his lap began, voice high and breathy. She slid her fingers into his hair and forced him to look at her. "You were gone for *so* long." She was beautiful and charming, that was for sure – jewel-toned eyes, long pale hair, an outfit Han was sure would result in some interesting tan lines when she stepped outside. And, hey, he was never going to shoot down the attentions of . . . a . . . uh . . . lady.

"Well, Sar – " he cut himself off when he saw the way her brows pulled together. Right. Sarla was the girl in Serenno Spaceport. Hellene was the Twi'lek barkeep at Kala'uun who had a thing for captains. Which meant this girl was . . .

Blank. Mos Eisley Spaceport Girl.

He shot her a charming, lopsided smile and stroked a knuckle down her cheek. "You know how it is. The jobs I get take me to every corner of the galaxy. Sometimes it's just too dangerous to show my face around the usual haunts. A guy like me" – he dropped his voice to a dramatic whisper – "he just has to keep moving."

The girl sighed. "Everyone's been talking about that spice cargo you had to dump. One of the freighter pilots said Jabba put a price on your head the size of this planet."

Han scowled. "This dust ball isn't *that* big."

She continued, ignoring him, her fingers moving to fiddle with the collar of his shirt. "You must have come back for a reason. A good one?"

Not a blonde one, he thought, reaching for his drink. Half paying attention to what the girl was saying, he scanned the cantina, searching for the kid and the old man – and found them, of course, right next to Chewie.

Leave it to the Wookiee to cozy right up to them, chatting them up like he hadn't just seen someone else get his fur singed. People only came into this particular cantina if they were looking to book a ship's services and weren't inclined to tell the Imperials about what they were transporting. Han's specialty.

But, really, he thought, what job was going to be worth letting a lunatic with a sword anywhere near his *Falcon*? They'd already had to turn down two measly jobs hauling goods off-planet. The pay was bad and the cargo was hot – literally steaming. Han might have taken a blow to his rep recently, but he had some professional pride left, thank you very much. One guy had wanted him to haul bantha dung into space to fertilise some other wasteland. No, thank you very much.

Chewbacca cut a path back towards Han's booth. If the almost two-and-a-half-meter-tall frame of shaggy brown hair didn't clear the way, the teeth and claws that completed the package did. Very few people knew Chewie had a mushy heart under that warrior's exterior.

The Wookiee looked at the girl in Han's lap, then at his friend, waiting. Han shrugged. What could he do? Some folks were just born irresistible.

But – hey, this was the opportunity he'd been waiting for. "Meet Chewbacca, my copilot. Chewie, meet . . ."

Han let his voice trail off, hoping she'd jump in and introduce herself. Instead, she pulled her head back, the way a serpent did right before it struck.

"Um . . . Allea?" he guessed.

Chewie groaned. The girl merely stood up,

picked up Han's drink, and threw the remainder in his face.

"It's Jenny," she said as she tossed her hair over her shoulder and stormed off.

Oh, *yeah* – Jenny from Mos Espa!

His copilot snickered as Han used his black vest to wipe his face off. The truth was, he did feel bad about his memory slip, not that he would show it.

"Laugh it up, buddy." Seeing Chewie's look, Han added, "Hey, you're the married one. Find me a human girl with Malla's brains and silky hair and maybe I'll consider it."

If a Wookiee could blush, Chewbacca would have been pink all over. He growled out a question.

Han sighed. "Yeah. I saw you with that old relic. Do I need to remind you he doesn't seem to like letting people keep their limbs?"

Chewie rumbled out a sharp response.

"Yeah, hard to miss the sword, pal. Of course I know what a lightsaber is. I wonder what antique trash heap he found it in."

The lightsaber was the chosen weapon of the Jedi Order, who served as peacekeepers in the Old Republic – pre-Emperor Palpatine's takeover. There was some religious mumbo jumbo about meditation and something called the Force. A great big wad of nonsense, if you asked Han. Their kind had been extinct so long they were practically ancient history.

"What's the job?" he asked. Chewie barked a response, and Han's eyes found the blonde kid again. The teen was fidgeting, looking around uncomfortably near the bar. Every now and then, he straightened his simple pale tunic. His hands were shaking so badly Han was surprised the little guppy didn't spill his drink.

"Passage?" Han repeated, turning back towards Chewie. "To the Alderaan system?" That was it? Usually when people wanted to hire a smuggler's ship, it was to disappear into restricted territory or one of the shadier hubs in the hopes of getting lost forever.

The Wookiee nodded.

"Think it'll pay well?"

OK. He had standards, but he also needed to pay back one of the galaxy's biggest crime lords. He could be flexible with his standards.

Chewie thumped the table as he snarled a response, going on and on about its being easy money. Finally, Han sighed and said, "Fine. Bring 'em over."

Han took a moment to straighten his vest and lean back in the booth, eyes scanning the cantina one last time for trouble. Chewie ushered the old man and the kid into seats across the table from him.

"Han Solo. I'm captain of the *Millennium Falcon*. Chewie here tells me you're looking for passage to the Alderaan system?"

"I'm Ben. This is Luke," the old man said, gesturing to the teenager. His calm presence was at complete odds with the kid's barely contained energy. Luke there looked like he was about to jump out of his skin, he was so eager to get going. "And, yes, indeed. If it's a fast ship."

Han scoffed. "Fast ship? You've never heard of the *Millennium Falcon*?"

Ben raised a white eyebrow. "Should I have?"

"It's the ship that made the Kessel Run in less than twelve parsecs!"

The kid, like most people who heard the tale, looked impressed. The old man was not, however, "most people."

"Anyway," Han said, before he could be called out on his lie. The *Falcon* was fast, and that was all that mattered. Point five past lightspeed was nothing to sniff at. "I've outrun Imperial starships. Not the local bulk cruisers, mind you. I'm talking about the big Corellian ships now. She's fast enough for you, old man. What's the cargo?"

Ben gave a thoughtful hum before answering. "Only passengers. Myself, the boy, two droids and no questions asked."

Suddenly, Han had a bad feeling about this job. "What is it? Some kind of local trouble?"

"Let's just say we'd like to avoid any Imperial entanglements."

"Well," Han said, leaning forwards. Oh, this was going to be *easy*. "That's the real trick, isn't it? And it's going to cost you something extra. Ten thousand, all in advance."

For the first time, the kid, Luke, spoke. "*Ten thousand?* We could almost buy our own ship for that!"

"Yeah, but who's going to fly it, kid? *You?*" He looked like he wouldn't be able to figure out how to retract the landing gear, never mind make a jump to hyperspace.

"You bet I could. I'm not such a bad pilot myself!" Luke turned towards Ben and started to stand, anger flaring hot and fast across his face. "We don't have to sit here and listen – "

The old man waved his hand, and the kid settled back into his seat. "We haven't that much with us. But we could pay you two thousand now, plus fifteen when we reach Alderaan."

Seventeen! Han wondered if he needed to clean his ears.

"OK, you guys got yourself a ship. We'll leave

as soon as you're ready. Docking bay ninety-four."

"Ninety-four," Ben repeated, nodding. Luke looked unhappy at the arrangement but managed to hold his tongue this time. Behind them, a flash of white caught Han's eye. Four uniformed stormtroopers were making their way up to the bar, attracting looks of scorn from the other patrons.

"Looks like someone's beginning to take an interest in your handiwork." Han tilted his head in the bar's direction.

His new passengers turned to look, the kid about jumping out of his skin as the barkeep pointed towards them. It was left to Ben to drag the kid off into the shadows, pulling him towards the back entrance. By the time the stormtroopers looked again, they were gone.

Han spun towards Chewie, gripping the silver bandolier across the Wookiee's chest. "*Seventeen thousand!* Those guys must be really desperate. Get back to the ship and get her ready."

The Wookiee slid out of the booth as Han signaled to the barkeep to close out his tab. Han fought the urge to sag in his seat in relief. The reasonable part of him knew it would only be a matter of time before he found a job to cover the cost of Jabba's lost cargo. But another part of him was starting to lose hope he'd get the credits in hand before a legit bounty hunter found him. It had been plain bad luck that an Imperial customs ship had crossed their path as they were preparing to leave Kessel with the illegal shipment. And now it was dumb luck that he could cover his rear.

Han stood, stretching out a kink in his neck. He took one step forwards, right into something hard, cold – something that felt suspiciously like the business end of a blaster. Then he heard in Huttese:

"Going somewhere, Solo?"

CHAPTER EIGHT

⊕

HAN FORCED A relaxed smile and turned slowly. The face that stared back at him was vivid green, covered in scales and bumps. Black glassy eyes sat atop a short trunk-like nose.

Greedo. In the grand scheme of bounty hunters and henchmen, the Rodian was about as dangerous as a fly buzzing around a bantha's bottom. Unfortunately, he was on the trigger-happy end of the spectrum of Jabba's hired help.

The captain slid back into the booth, relaxing in his seat. If he showed a hint of nerves around the cretin, even with a gun pointed at him, Han would never forgive himself.

"As a matter of fact," he told the Rodian, "I was just about to go see your boss. But now *you* can tell Jabba that I've got his money."

"It's too late," Greedo said, a little too happily for Han's liking. "You should have paid him when you had the chance. Jabba's put a price on your head so large that every bounty hunter in the galaxy will be looking for you. I'm lucky I found you first."

Han was lucky, too. If it had been a reputable bounty hunter – say, Boba Fett – he would have been in a galaxy of trouble. Still, he wasn't sure if Jabba's contract on his life had the "dead or alive" clause, so he wasn't about to go shooting off his mouth. "Yeah, but this time I got the money."

"If you give it to me, I might forget I found you. . . ." Greedo leaned across the table. He would have winked if he had a sense of humour.

"I don't have it with me. Look, it was a little thing, getting boarded. . . ." Han slowly reached for his gun under the table, sliding it from the holster at his hip. His fingers brushed against the cool metal as he sucked in a lungful of the cantina's warm smoky air.

"You can tell that to Jabba," Greedo said. "He may only take your ship."

Now it was Han's turn to sneer. "Over my dead body!"

The Rodian laughed, the sound trumpeting out of his snout as he trained his gun right on Han's heart. "That's the idea. I've been looking forwards to killing you for a long time."

A slow smile spread across the captain's face. "Yeah. I'll bet you have."

Greedo disappeared in a blinding flash of white light as Han pulled the trigger on his gun. The thump as Greedo's body slumped onto the table made the other cantina patrons look over.

Poor Greedo, Han thought, glancing down at the smoking corpse as he stood again. Never realised Han could shoot under a table just as well as above it.

"I said *no blasters!*" the barkeep growled.

"For your trouble." Han reached into his pocket and flipped him a coin. "Sorry about the mess."

He couldn't get out of that cantina fast enough. The hot wall of desert air slammed into him as he stepped outside. *Like walking into an oven,* he thought, shielding his eyes from the sun beating down over-head. The dust flying through the air was thick that day. An unusual number of stormtroopers were kicking it up in the unpaved streets, dirtying their pristine white uniforms. Soon they'd blend in with the tan, sun-bleached buildings around them.

Now he had a *really* bad feeling about the job.

And that feeling only got worse when he saw Chewie hovering outside the hangar door and heard a deep voice calling to him in Huttese: *"Come out, Solo!"*

His copilot glanced back at him, hearing his boots shuffling through the loose sand.

"Didn't want to go in alone?" Han asked, pat-ting Chewie's shoulder. "I don't blame you. Let's get it over with."

"Solo!"

Slithering along the ground like the slug he was, Jabba waited outside the *Millennium Falcon*, shouting for Han. A half dozen of Jabba's hench-men circled the ship. Han crossed his arms over his chest, counting the weapons strapped to each of the thugs. Jabba seemed to be starting a collection of the system's ugliest – with himself as the crown jewel.

Han had told Chewie his theory once that, unlike the other life forms, the Hutts hadn't evolved from sparks of life and matter; the galaxy had simply belched them out one day. As long as Han was tall, and carrying about five times Han's weight, the Hutt was a putrid combination of brown-and-yellowing-green skin. All warts and wrinkles and a drooling tongue he seemed incapable of keeping inside his mouth.

"I've been waiting for you, Jabba," Han said, letting his voice echo through the hangar. When Jabba and the others turned, Han felt his stomach flip. The Hutt's gold reptile-like eyes tracked Han's movements as he came closer.

"I expected you would be," Jabba answered.

"I'm not the type to run." Well, a solid 60 percent of the time he wasn't.

Jabba liked to talk to him as if Han were his wayward son. Han let him, because Han enjoyed keeping his life. "Han, my boy, there are times when you disappoint me. . . . Why haven't you paid me? And why did you have to fry poor Greedo like that?"

News travelled fast, it seemed.

"You sent Greedo to blast me," Han reminded him.

Those gold eyes widened in fake shock. "You're the best smuggler in the business. You're too valuable to fry. He was only relaying . . . my *concern* at your delays. He wasn't going to blast you."

Han waved a hand dismissively. "If you've got something to say to me, come see me yourself."

"Han, Han!" Jabba let out one of his belly laughs, the same kind he gave as he fed slaves to his pet rancor. "You're my favourite scoundrel, don't you know? You and I are alike. We love money – the smell of it, the feel of it, the weight of it in our pockets. I understand you better than you think."

Han recoiled at the thought that he was anything like the slug in front of him.

"If only you hadn't had to dump that shipment

of spice . . ." Jabba continued. "You understand I can't make an exception. Where would I be if all of my smugglers dumped their shipment at the first sign of an Imperial starship? It's not good for business."

"I had no choice, but I've got a charter now and I can pay you back, plus a little extra. I just need some time." Han held up his hands. "C'mon. How long have I been running for you? And this is the first time I've had to ditch the cargo?"

Jabba seemed to consider that. "For an extra, say . . . twenty percent, I'll give you a little more time . . . but this is it. If you disappoint me again, I'll put a price on your head so large you won't be able to go near a civilised system for the rest of your short life."

Han gave a little bow, then expertly talked the crime lord down to 15 percent. "Always a pleasure to do business with you."

Jabba was still laughing as he slithered out of the hangar, the others trailing behind him like faithful pets. Han's stomach didn't unclench until

Jabba was gone from sight, and Chewie let out a relieved rumble from deep in his chest.

"You said it," Han said. "Think he would have sold us into slavery or just sent us shooting out into the vacuum of space to watch us pop into little splats?"

Neither of which would be the worst of what the Hutt had done. What Jabba lacked in looks he made up for in endless creativity in hiding the bodies of his enemies.

Han mopped the sweat off the back of his neck and shuddered. "All right, time to get down to work. Let's get her ready to fly."

It felt good to get back in the swing of things. He and Chewie ran through all the usual preflight checks, recalibrating some of the instruments and charting the course they'd take to the Alderaan system. Han was lovingly polishing one of the control panels when he heard someone cry, "What a piece of *junk*!"

The kid, of course. Clearly that one was fresh off the moisture farm if he couldn't recognise the beauty of the *Falcon*'s fine lines. The YT series was the height of Corellian engineering genius. A *triumph*. Maybe she was getting on in age . . . and some of her plates didn't match . . . and maybe he hadn't been able to paint over some of the worst scorch marks – but so what? It was what was inside that counted most.

Han didn't have much good in his life; aside from Chewie, his ship was the only thing he could count on in a real fight. She was the love of his life, had been from the moment he won her from another scoundrel in a game of cards. And if the sand rat didn't stop insulting her, he was going to find himself blasted back down to Tatooine in an escape pod.

Han walked down the boarding ramp to meet them. "She'll make point five beyond the speed of light. She may not look like much, but she's got it where it counts, kid. I've added some special modifications myself."

Luke scratched his head, shooting the old man an uncertain look. Han closed his eyes and counted to ten. Seventeen thousand, he reminded himself. If it was a choice between Jabba slowly feeding pieces of him to a pit of acid or dealing with a little punk, he could deal with the punk.

"We're a little rushed," Han said, sweeping his hands towards the ramp, "so if you'll hurry aboard we'll get out of here."

Trailing behind the humans were two droids: one a golden humanoid protocol droid who shuffled forwards on stiff limbs and surveyed the hangar with round glowing eyes, the other a white cylindrical astromech droid on three legs, with a silver domed head and blue detailing. Its small alert light flashed blue and red as it swivelled its head around. Both looked like they'd been rolling around the dunes for days.

Han waited until they were all on board before starting up the ramp behind them. He cast one last look over his shoulder. One more trip back. After he got his money, he'd make one final trip to that pit to deliver it to Jabba. And then he'd make sure to keep a few systems between him and the Hutt.

"Stop that ship!"

Han did a double take, spinning around. The thunder of feet and clattering armour was his only warning before stormtroopers poured into the hangar. Their blaster rifles were already up.

"Blast 'em!" the one out front ordered.

Han swore in three different languages as he ducked up the ramp, chased by bolts of energy burning the air around him. He turned back and fired with his own blaster. Throwing himself up through the overhead door, he slammed his palm against its release button. The stormtroopers' shots glanced off the *Millennium Falcon*'s shields.

"Chewie!" Han called as he rushed past the holding area. He glanced around to make sure their passengers were buckling in. "Get us out of here!"

His copilot roared back from the cockpit, drowning out the protocol droid's snooty, "Oh my, I'd forgotten how much I hate space travel!"

The *Falcon* was already clear of the hangar by the time Han collapsed into the pilot's seat, his hands flying across the console. They rose above the dingy, sand-whipped buildings of Mos Eisley, heading into the early afternoon sky. It never got old, seeing the way the sky purpled and darkened as they blasted out of the atmosphere. *That* was why Han loved flying.

And pulling off a narrow escape wasn't such a bad feeling, either.

Han had barely sat down in the pilot's chair next to Chewie when the Wookiee pointed to the sensor scope, growling out a warning.

Han's stomach clenched at the sight of the large blip rapidly approaching them as they broke clear of Tatooine's atmosphere and entered the black gaping mouth of outer space.

"Looks like an Imperial cruiser," he said with a grimace. "Our passengers must be hotter than I thought. Try and hold them off. Angle the deflector shield while I make the calculations for the jump to lightspeed."

As his hands flew over the navigation console, Han was vaguely aware of the silver-and-blue astromech droid rolling past the open cockpit door, beeping out what sounded like a few questions. Ignored, he rolled away, headed towards Luke and Ben to slip into a small space beside Threepio.

Luke and Ben made their way into the cramped cockpit, where Han was continuing his calculations. Great. Now he had an audience.

"Stay sharp," he warned Chewie. "It looks like we have two more Imperial ships coming in. They're going to try to cut us off before we can make the jump to hyperspace."

His copilot shot him an irritated look, clearly already two steps ahead of him. What could he say? One Imperial Star Destroyer, about fifty times the size of the *Falcon*, was enough to make him a little nervous. Three made him downright jumpy.

Luke leaned forwards for a better look. "Why don't you outrun them? I thought you said this thing was fast!"

What was that, the fourth time the kid had insulted his baby?

"Watch your mouth, kid, or you're going to find

yourself *floating* home! We'll be safe enough once we make the jump to hyperspace. Besides, I know a few manoeuvres." More to himself than the others he promised, "We'll lose them!"

The *Millennium Falcon* bucked wildly at the first hits from the Imperial cruisers. White-blue sparks flashed outside the viewport, but the shields held.

"Here's where the fun begins!" he told the others. Adrenaline pumped through him, filling his chest like a balloon.

"How long before you can make the jump to lightspeed?" The old man was the calm eye at the centre of a storm. His pale blue eyes watched the sea of stars in front of him. He didn't seem particularly bothered even as the ship shuddered and rocked around them, like it was on the verge of exploding.

"It'll take a few moments to get the coordinates from the navicomputer."

"Are you kidding?" Luke cried. "At the rate they're gaining . . . ?"

Good thing he didn't finish that thought. Han

glared at him. This kid, honestly.

"Travelling through hyperspace ain't like dusting crops, boy!" he said. "Without precise calculations we could fly right through a star or bounce too close to a supernova, and that'd end your trip real quick, wouldn't it?"

The fire from the Star Destroyers came fast and hot now that Chewie could no longer avoid the bulk of it. Han braced a hand against the side paneling of the cockpit and input the last of the new coordinates. A red light flashed overhead, beeping out warning after warning after warning. Han winced.

"What does that flashing mean?" Luke asked.

"We're, uh, losing our deflector shield. Go strap yourself in – I'm going to make the jump to lightspeed."

And not a second too soon. Han met Chewbacca's light eyes. "Punch it."

The stars brightened around them, flaring to life in the second before the ship picked up speed. He was pushed back against his seat as the *Falcon* flew forwards into hyperspace, leaving the

Imperial cruisers to eat its dust. Han let out an exhilarated laugh.

OK, so maybe *that* was the best part of flying.

CHAPTER NINE

"**T**HAT'S IT, EXACTLY. The Force is what gives a Jedi his power. It's an energy field created by all living things. It surrounds us and penetrates us; it binds the galaxy together."

Han's fingers slowed from where he was patching some of the *Falcon*'s fried wiring. The whole ship had taken a battering during their narrow escape from the Star Destroyers, and he had kept busy seeing to fixing it.

Meanwhile, the old man had been lecturing Luke from the moment the ship had settled into hyperspace. They, Chewie and the droids had migrated from the cockpit to the central hold area. Han told himself he was only hanging around nearby to make sure they didn't get any ideas about throwing their lightsabers around.

He lifted his protective mask and cut the welding gun to watch their reflections in a nearby panel. The old man was still trying to teach the kid to hold his sword and had moved on to posing Luke like a toy doll. Ben adjusted the kid's stance, pushing his legs out farther and having him raise his arms just so. Han wasn't convinced one needed perfect technique when one had a sword that could cut through just about anything.

"Like this, Luke," Ben said, swinging his own lightsaber hilt down, then back up, then back down. Han was grateful Ben wasn't working with his blade ignited like the kid was, otherwise the ship would be in pieces. "Block, strike, block – yes, precisely. Do you feel the Force moving through you? It guides your body and obeys your command in equal measure."

"Yeah," Luke said. "Yeah, I mean, I think I feel *something*. . . ."

Uh-huh. Hacking at the air for a half hour was going to give you sore arms, but that was about it.

"Wonderful." Ben shifted, sliding his foot back, raising his lightsaber hilt again, and tilting his wrists back. "Strike position. Relax your grip slightly. This leaves your chest open to attack, so you must only hold this position for no more than a moment."

Luke arched his back, and the pose was so strange Han couldn't keep his chuckle in. The kid must have heard it because he scowled and switched the lightsaber off. "Oh, this is *pointless*. What can I really learn on a ship in a few hours?"

Exactly. Han dropped his mask back down over his face and returned to the circuitry in front of him.

"I do not expect you to master everything in mere minutes, and you should not expect that of yourself, either. That is a path to frustration, anger – and both are dangerous."

As he switched the welder off again, Han heard Luke ask, "What do you mean?"

"There are two sides of the Force," Ben continued. "The light side of the Force, the way of the Jedi, aligns with selflessness, enlightenment, mercy, and compassion. The dark side, the way of the Sith, deals in hatred, fear, anger, jealousy. You must learn to control your emotions, otherwise they will control you."

Ha! Han thought. *Easier said than done.* Wasn't the mix of all that what made them humans?

"Why do some go to the dark side?" he heard Luke ask. "If they know that it brings destruction and pain, what's the draw?"

"Everyone has their own destinies," the old man said. "The Force works in mysterious ways, but it leads us to where we need to be in order to achieve balance. Many Sith believe that the dark side holds more power, but that is simply not true."

Han strained his ears to catch what the old man said next.

"It was the Force that brought me into your life, and it is the Force that will guide you to your destiny."

It *was* a comforting thought, even Han had to

admit – the idea that everything happened for a reason. But the part about not being in the pilot seat of his own life rubbed at him in a bad way. And he knew firsthand that "good" and "evil" were not as cut-and-dry as the old loon was making them sound. Most people, himself included, had to live in that narrow, fuzzy bit of grey in between. Because what ensured a long life tended to be good aim with a blaster, a fast ship, and dependable friends – not hoping some big energy field had your back.

Everyone was just living and trying to get by in bad situations. Why should Han be any different? He sat up a little straighter, shaking his head. From an early age, he'd learned always to rely on himself to decide his future, and nothing was going to change that now. All these causes people got behind – the Force, even the new Rebel Alliance – they only led straight to tragedy. Han had seen enough of life to know that, too.

The kid continued to slide between stances,

blocking and striking at an invisible enemy. Han was so busy pretending he wasn't watching, he missed the R2 unit rolling up behind him until the thing knocked into him and whistled to get his attention.

"You finished scanning the hyperdrive? Everything look good?" Han asked.

The R2 unit whistled an affirmative and rolled past him before Han could ask about the sensor transceiver. The floor paneling rattled as the droid's wheels moved over it, taking the droid into the central hold. Han was about to turn back to lock up the circuit panel when he saw the fossil wave the droid over. Luke had a look of intense concentration on his face as he pivoted around and around in a circle, lifting his lightsaber this way, that way, clearly lost in his own world.

The R2 unit moved to Ben's side as if it were his faithful pet – an image that was further reinforced by the old man's stroking a hand over its domed head.

"It's good to fly with you again, my old friend,"

the old man said, so softly Han wasn't sure he had heard him right. But it wasn't Han's business either way. He knelt down to pile his tools into their box and went back to his work.

"Ben!" he heard Luke say. "Are you all right? What's wrong?"

Han leaned back again, peering into the central hold area. The old man swayed on his feet, pressing a hand to his white hair. "I felt . . . a great disturbance in the Force. It was as if millions of voices suddenly cried out in terror and were . . . silenced. I fear something terrible has happened."

Han gave up pretending not to be listening and made his way inside the cramped space.

"Well," he said, to lighten the mood, "you can forget your troubles with those Imperial slugs. I told you I'd outrun 'em."

The kid had his lightsaber in his hands and was squaring off with a fist-sized seeker droid Han used for target practice. It floated and bobbed in the air. Past it, Chewie was locked in his own battle. He faced the little astromech droid across the Dejarik board, focused on the small holographic monsters on the table between them. He made his move. A monster clobbered one of the droid's across the board.

"Don't everyone thank me at once," Han said dryly.

"Now be careful, Artoo . . ." the protocol droid began as Han took a seat.

The R2 droid reached out a little claw hand and tapped his screen. One of his creatures moved to a new square. Chewie's temper flared and he began shouting in Wookiee at the droid.

"He made a fair move!" The golden droid said, and Han honestly thought he would have wagged a finger at the Wookiee if he physically could. "Screaming about it won't help you."

"Let him have it. It's not wise to upset a Wookiee." Han crossed his arms over his chest, brows raised.

"But, sir," the droid protested, "no one worries about upsetting a droid."

"That's 'cause droids don't pull people's arms out of their socket when they lose."

The protocol droid's round eyes flashed. "I see your point, sir. I suggest a new strategy, Artoo. Let the Wookiee win."

The R2 unit whistled in protest, but Han had already turned his attention to where Luke was standing at the centre of the hold, lightsaber humming in his hands.

"Remember, a Jedi can *feel* the Force flowing through him," Ben said.

"So . . . it controls my actions?" Luke asked, clearly confused.

"Partially. But it also obeys your commands."

The seeker droid floated to one side of Luke, then lunged to the other, as if taunting him. It flew back and made another fast-as-lightning move behind him. Han caught himself holding his breath as he watched. A bright laser bolt flew out of the seeker droid, nailing Luke in the leg. The kid tumbled over with a squawk of alarm.

Han laughed . . . and laughed. Of course.

"Hokey religions and ancient weapons are no match for a good weapon at your side."

And the old man's methods had just proven that all over again.

Luke turned to Han. "You don't believe in the Force, do you?"

Wasn't that obvious? "I've flown from one side of this galaxy to the other. I've seen *a lot* of strange stuff, but I've never seen anything to make me believe there's one all-powerful 'Force' controlling everything. There's no mystical energy field that controls *my* destiny."

Instead of glaring at Han or trying to start an argument Han was more than ready for, the old man merely smiled.

"It's just a lot of tricks and nonsense," Han insisted.

The old man rose to his feet, smoothing his brown robes as he searched the hold for something. Ah – a helmet.

"I suggest you try it again, Luke," he said, placing the large white helmet on the kid's head. Its blast shield was down, effectively blinding him.

"I can't even see," Luke said, laughing. "How am I supposed to fight?"

"Your eyes can deceive you. Don't trust them."

Han rolled his eyes at the old man's words. This was going to be good.

The remote shot straight up into the air, resetting. Luke swung the sword around so blindly, Han almost jumped between the blue lightsaber and the tender walls of his ship. But the seeker got there first, this time sending a bolt of hot laser right into Luke's behind. Han almost fell out of his chair laughing as the poor kid yelped.

"Stretch out with your feelings," Ben said, undaunted. "Luke, you can do this. Trust your instincts."

To Han's surprise, Luke squared his shoulders and stood in position again. His hands were steady as they held the lightsaber. Even Chewie and the droids turned to watch. But no matter how many times the seeker droid bopped around the kid, clearly trying to bait him into turning or dodging,

Luke stayed still. Han was so focused on watching Luke that the sudden zap of energy from the droid startled him.

But not Luke. The kid swung the sword around expertly, deflecting the red bolt. Han's eyes widened. And when he pulled off the helmet, Luke looked like even he couldn't believe it.

Ben clapped his hands. "You see? You can do it!"

"I call it luck," Han muttered, crossing his arms over his chest. It was one thing to do it against a remote-controlled droid and a whole other game to do it against the living.

"In my experience, there's no such thing as luck," Ben said as he rose stiffly onto his feet. "How much longer until we reach the Alderaan system?"

Despite his obvious pleasure at the kid's finally scoring one against the seeker droid, Han could see the old man's face was still pale. Han could tell there was something stirring beneath the calm waters of his exterior.

"About twenty minutes?" Han guessed. "If you need to take a load off, there's a bunk in the back."

"Much appreciated," Ben said with a nod.

"Third door on your left," Han called after him, craning his neck to watch as the old man disappeared.

Chewie was grumbling about some move the droid had made when Han turned to look at Luke. The kid was practising some of the moves Ben had shown him earlier, clearly envisioning himself as the lone hero in some great battle.

It occurred to Han that he didn't know the first thing about the kid, other than that he'd ticked off someone in the Imperial forces. *Been there,* Han thought. It irritated him, his curiosity about Luke. How he could still be so . . . energetic about the idea of being part of some bigger force. So much of Han's own survival had depended on evading questions that he'd lived under the philosophy of "ask no questions, get no lies" for years. He didn't ask people about themselves because he didn't want them to ask *him* questions he couldn't or wouldn't answer.

But just like that, Han found himself breaking his own rule. "So, is he your grandfather or something?"

Luke's bright blue eyes flashed. "Ben? He's a great man, you know. A Jedi Master."

Han snorted. Or so the old man said. "That's not what I asked."

"Oh, no. But he knew my father. They fought together in the Clone Wars. He's the one who gave me my father's old lightsaber." Luke held it up for Han to inspect.

"Nice." Han pushed against the feeling of anger balling in the pit of his stomach. He couldn't claim very many honourable qualities, but not trying to pull anything over on impressionable youth was one of them. He only took advantage of people who deserved it, thank you very much.

"But why couldn't dear ol' Dad give it to you himself?"

Luke's expression darkened, and Han

suddenly felt like the biggest pile of rancor poodoo. Right. If Ben's story was true, it meant Luke's father had been a Jedi. And the Jedi were gone. Hunted and killed as Emperor Palpatine rose to power.

"Both he and my mother died when I was a baby," Luke explained. "I grew up on Tatooine with my Uncle Owen and Aunt Beru."

Wow. He really *was* fresh off the moisture farm. "And they let you go off on this joy ride?"

Chewie roared in victory, slamming his furry fists down on the game board. If Han had glanced away, he would have missed the flash of sharp, deep pain cross Luke's face. "No . . . they were . . ." he struggled with the words. "They were murdered. By the Empire."

Scratch that. As Luke told him everything that had happened back on Tatooine, Han felt like the biggest *steaming* pile of rancor poodoo in *the history of the galaxy*.

"Geez, kid . . ." Han said when Luke had finished. He rubbed the back of his neck. "Let me see if I got this straight. You and your uncle bought those two droids off Jawas, and it turns out the short one has something stored on it the Empire wants? Then he runs off, claiming he's owned by a Ben Kenobi. You chase him, barely survive a Sand People attack, and then *willingly* follow the fossil back to his home. Which is a cave. Where he has lived alone for twenty years. With only his make-believe stories about Jedi to keep him company."

Luke nodded, clearly not getting what was wrong with that picture. Han stared at him, waiting. Apparently he was going to be waiting forever.

"You realise you've put all your faith in a crazy person . . . right?"

"Ben is *not* crazy! I meant what I said – I felt the Force earlier. He hasn't lied to me. He wouldn't."

Oh, boy. Han patted Luke's shoulder as he stood. "Stick with me, kid. I'll do you better than trying to tie you to some mystic energy. I'll teach you how to *survive*."

A faint alarm echoed over to them from the

cockpit. "Looks like we're coming up on Alderaan. Better go wake your friend up from his beauty sleep."

Han took the pilot's seat again. Chewie ducked into the cockpit a moment later, taking the chair next to Han's.

"All right, here we go," Han said. "Stand by for hyperspace exit."

He reached over to a lever on the console in front of him, pulling it back in a slow, smooth motion. The stars racing by in smears of white light suddenly solidified into points.

And then the *Falcon* began to shudder, violently tossing back and forth. "What the – ?"

Spread out in front of them was a field of small asteroids, all of which seemed to be racing straight towards the *Falcon*. Han's heart slammed against his ribs as he seized the controls and yanked left, spinning the ship away from the hunk of space rocks flying straight for the cockpit. The ship dipped and twirled between the dark rocks as nimble as any dancer, so fast that even *he* felt a little dizzy. A small piece of asteroid slammed into the ship's hull and ricocheted off, sending an *even bigger* asteroid hurtling towards them. Han tugged the controls back. The *Falcon* shot straight up before looping back down. The ship missed the big asteroid by mere metres.

It was the hardest workout either he or the ship had gotten in some time. He didn't breathe easily until they broke through the thick of it and were bouncing through just fragments and shards like bad turbulence.

Chewie tossed out his theory in a growling snarl.

Han nodded. "Yeah, it must be some kind of meteor shower – an asteroid collision. It's not on any of the charts."

Luke stumbled into the cockpit, barely catching himself on the door before he fell through it. "What's going on?"

Han scratched his head, his face scrunching in thought as he double-checked the charts. "Our position is correct, except . . . no Alderaan."

"What do you mean? Where is it?" Luke demanded, dropping into one of the seats behind them. Han glanced back just as old Ben came in and sat down next to the boy.

"That's what I'm trying to tell you, kid. It's been totally blown away."

"What?" Luke gasped. *How?*

"Destroyed," Ben said, his quiet voice almost lost under the banging of rocky debris against the ship's hull. "By the Empire."

The old man *had* lost it. "The entire starfleet couldn't destroy the whole planet. It'd take a thousand ships with more firepower than I've – "

Han was interrupted by a whining *beep-beep-beep* from the console. "There's another ship coming in."

"Maybe they'll know what happened?" Luke offered, leaning forwards for a better look.

"No, it's an Imperial fighter," Ben said. "Look at the shape – the flat wings bookending the round cockpit. That's a TIE fighter."

Chewie barked out a note of concern as the

Imperial ship screeched over their heads.

"It followed us!" Luke said. "How is that possible?"

"No, those are short-range fighters," Ben said. "It couldn't have."

"There aren't any bases around here, at least not that I'm aware of," Han said, glancing back at Ben. "You know something I don't?"

The TIE fighter raced towards what looked like a star in the near distance.

"If they identify us, we're in trouble," Luke said. Like Han wasn't already *well* aware of that concern.

"Not if I can help it," Han said. "Chewie, jam its transmissions."

"It'd be as well to let it go," Ben said. "It's too far out of range."

"Well, he won't be around long enough to tell anyone about us," Han said, pushing the *Millennium Falcon* until she began to rattle in protest. "Let's get him in range to fire on."

Luke squinted, practically on top of Han now

as he leaned towards the viewport window. "I thought it was a star, but it . . . looks almost like a moon?"

But that couldn't be right, either. . . . Han swivelled in his seat, glancing at his navigation charts again. Alderaan had no moon, and – It was just for a moment, but Han was sure his heart up and froze on him. Because they were close enough now, closer than Han should have ever allowed them to get. He could see the surface of the silvery moon wasn't pockmarked with craters or mountains or even dried sea beds. It was metal. All of it, metal. The skin of the thing was textured by towers, panelling, and the deep ravines among them.

Han had flown to every corner of the galaxy, slipped through its grimy cracks, seen stars explode, and brushed up against death, close enough to feel its icy breath. But for the first time in a long, long while, he was too stunned to speak.

It was the old man who finally put words to Han's thoughts.

"That's no moon," Ben said. "It's a space station."

CHAPTER TEN

"**I HAVE A** *very* bad feeling about this," Luke said slowly. He was still blinking, as if he could erase the sight.

"Yeah, I think you're right," Han said. He turned to Chewie. "Lock in the auxiliary power – "

The *Millennium Falcon* gave a sharp jerk, as if it had slammed into an invisible wall. Han gave the controls a tug, reaching up to try to adjust the power, but they were already flying at full speed. A prickle of panic ran down his spine before he could stamp it out.

"Why are we still moving towards it?" Luke asked.

"We're caught in a tractor beam," Han said, struggling to control his outrage. "There's nothing I can do. It's pulling us in."

Right into the open hangar of the enormous battle station. They were taking his ship. The Imperials were actually taking the *Falcon*, and this time he had a feeling they weren't going to let him and Chewie off with a slap on the wrist. He swivelled in his seat, resentment steaming through him as he looked from a dumbstruck Luke to an unruffled Ben. They should never have taken this job.

Forget the money. The *Falcon* was all Han had to his name. And unless he could think on his feet, he wouldn't even have that.

"They're not going to get me without a fight," he told the others, facing forwards again. A hand settled lightly on his shoulder.

"You can't win," Ben said. "But there are alternatives to fighting. Tell me, are there smuggling compartments on this ship?"

Han raised an eyebrow. "Know many successful smugglers without them?"

Chewie barked out a nervous question as the ship was tugged towards the gaping mouth of the open hangar.

"No, I know what he's getting at," Han said, putting a steadying hand on his copilot's arm. As much as he hated to admit it, Tatooine's twin suns hadn't completely dried out the old man's brain. "Go open the compartments and get everyone inside. I'll take care of things up here."

"You might want to jettison escape pods," Ben said as Chewie stood and started to usher them out of the cockpit.

"Do you know how expensive those are to replace?" Han asked, outraged.

"More or less valuable than your life?" was the calm response.

Han was still muttering about old men and their stupid questions when he turned back to the console and went to work writing up a quick notation in the captain's log. *Abandoned ship upon entering the Alderaan system due to safety concerns.* With a resigned sigh, he launched the empty escape pods. He listened to the pop and hiss as their restraints released and sent them spiraling into space.

His escape pods. From *his* ship. The one he'd won

in a perfect stroke of luck during a game of cards. The one he'd spent years modifying and repairing. The one that had never let him down, not when it counted. Han wasted a few moments watching the battle station edge closer and closer. He powered down the ship and turned sharply on his heel, his boots clicking softly as he made his way back towards the others.

His ship. The *Millennium Falcon* already had quite a record to her name in just smuggling charges. Han had never claimed to be the brightest star twinkling in the sky, but he could put two and two together. Being tied to the Empire's hunt for those droids would sink both him and his ship. If – no, *when*, they got out of this, he would need to repaint her, alter her appearance, give her a new name. It was that or . . . buy a new ship. But that thought was like a laser blast to the chest.

He couldn't give up on her. So many people had given up on Han – he couldn't do that to his ship.

The smuggling compartments were hidden beneath the floor of one of the ship's narrow hallways. The latch to release them was virtually invisible if you didn't know where to look. Chewie had left one of the floor plates up for him.

"How close do you think we are?" he heard Luke ask.

"Too close." Han crouched down, peering into the cramped space before sliding inside. The compartment was so shallow he had to crouch down to fit. Chewie must have been folded in half or curled on his side. When Han turned, he got a mouthful of Wookiee hair.

Well, well, well. Smuggling himself on his own ship. This was definitely a first. One of them had the thought to power off the droids, at least, though the protocol droid's foot was wedged into his back.

"Ouch, that was my knee!" Luke cried

Chewie rumbled out a low apology.

"Quiet now," Ben said. "We should be passing into the docking bay momentarily."

Luke let out a small gasp of surprise as the ship dropped sharply once and then again. The second drop rattled them around like dice in a cup.

A deafening screech of metal against metal made Han wince. The ship had all but belly flopped onto the hangar floor. He hadn't been able to deploy the landing gear without giving them away.

Finally, someone must have gotten control of the cockpit remotely, because the ship rose on its landing gear. The ship's boarding ramp creaked as it was lowered. To distract himself, Han started mentally adding up the astronomical cost of repairs. But once the troops flooded in, their boots pounding the floor and their voices buzzing out commands, they were impossible to ignore.

"Search this ship! Every centimeter of it!"

"The escape pods have been deployed, sir!"

"The captain's log indicates they abandoned ship."

The sickening thought of Imperial filth tracking their dirt into his ship faded as realisation set in. The stormtroopers must have passed right over them a dozen times, and never once did they seem to stop or slow. They were going to get away with it.

All that was left to do was wait.

CHAPTER ELEVEN

─────────────── ✪ ───────────────

HAN KEPT HIS back flat against the wall next to the ship's open hatch, risking another glance down the ramp. The cool, fresh oxygen made him feel alert. The compartment had grown so warm Han had felt smothered by the damp air.

He glanced over to where Chewie stood on the other side of the door, giving him a small signal. His copilot pulled back, ducking farther into the ship. Han was about to follow when his attention was drawn back to the two stormtroopers stationed at the bottom of the boarding ramp.

"The ship's all yours," one of the stormtroopers called. A moment later, a small group of men from the hangar crew appeared. They pushed a large, dark-blue rectangular cart forwards. Han recognised it immediately – a scanner. So those white helmets weren't empty after all. They would scan every centimeter of the ship looking for hidden compartments.

"If the scanners pick up anything, report it immediately," the stormtrooper said.

Han fell back, moving quickly to where Chewie was waiting around the nearest corner. Luke and Ben hovered a short distance behind him. The kid was the very picture of nerves. Han gave him a reassuring look before setting his blaster to stun.

Han tracked the sound of the scanner crew as they entered the *Falcon* and set to turning on the machine. The three men spoke quietly to each other as they started their work, rolling the scanner forwards – right into the waiting Wookiee. The crew had one second to look terrified before Chewie knocked two out with his fists and Han stunned the third into a deep sleep.

Han cupped his hands around his mouth and called, "Hey, down there! Could you give us a hand with this?"

He had to give them a little credit – both storm-troopers were quick reaching for their guns, but very few in the galaxy were faster on the draw than Han. The two stormtroopers fell just as hard as the scanner crew did.

"Nice shooting," Luke said, clapping Han on the shoulder.

"Thanks, kid. Now, which one do you want?" Han gestured to the two stormtroopers.

"Quickly, quickly," Ben said, keeping an eye on the boarding ramp as Luke and Han stripped the stormtroopers of their uniforms.

"Oh *my*!" The protocol droid, C-3PO, as Luke called him, sounded startled at being rebooted. The R2 unit rolled around them, investigating what they were doing.

"Phew," Han said, holding out the black fabric jumpsuit. "You think these guys ever heard of bathing? Mine smells like the guy slept in it."

Luke took a sniff of his, then groaned. "I think they must have served something spicy for lunch today."

Han threw the stiff white armour on, adjusting the various straps. The helmet smelled like bad breath. "Lead on, old man. This is your plan."

Ben's dark brown robe swept out behind him as he made his way down the ramp.

Han glanced over his shoulder, telling Luke, "We need to keep the droids behind us – "

Something clattered in the distance, and a faint *whomp-whomp-whomp* alarm sounded. Han ran down the steps just in time to see the remaining stormtroopers and hangar crew rushing through the exit. Ben stood in the shadows of the *Falcon*, his hood up.

"What did you do?" Han asked.

"Tricks and nonsense," Ben said with a small smile. "A security alarm required their attention."

Han was still staring at Ben when Luke and Chewie followed the old man out.

"Let's go," Luke said, nodding towards the glass observation window two stories above them. The small command centre would give them access to the battle station's technical details. If Ben was right, they might be able to disable the tractor beam from there.

They had no problems entering the elevator unseen, riding it up to the third level in silence. The door slid open, and Han stepped out first, narrowly avoiding the troop of officers marching by.

Ben said quietly, "I believe it's that door over there."

"All right, let's get this over with." Han led the way, getting into position just outside the door, Luke and Chewie to his right. Before he could buzz to be let in, the door snapped open. The Imperial officer standing there jumped back in alarm, just as Chewie let out a magnificent roar.

Han fired on the other officer manning the switchboards and controls, taking him out as the rest of their group flooded into the room behind him.

"You know," Luke said as he ripped off his helmet, "between his howling and your blasting everything in sight, it's a wonder the whole station doesn't know we're here!"

"Bring them on!" Han shot back, taking off his own helmet. "I prefer a straight fight to all of this sneaking around."

Luke was still shaking his head when he turned to Ben. "Are you all right? You look like you've seen a ghost."

The old man had turned back towards the door they'd come through, his head cocked slightly to the side as if he were listening to something the rest of them couldn't hear. "I sensed a presence I've not felt in some time. . . ."

"We found the computer outlet, sir," Threepio said. "He says he's found the main computer to power the tractor beam that's holding the ship. He'll try to make the precise location appear on the monitor."

Han hadn't even seen the little R2 unit stick its little probe arm into one of the sockets of the console. While he and Luke went to watch the monitor, Han, actually using his head, turned and secured the locks on the doors.

"The tractor beam is coupled to the main reactor

in seven locations," Threepio explained, ignoring the whistles from the R2 unit. "A power loss at one of these terminals will allow the ship to leave."

Ben studied the map on the screen. "I don't think you boys can help with this. I must go alone."

Great. Fantastic. Han held up his hands. "Whatever you say. You aren't paying me nearly enough for this."

Luke ignored Han, grabbing Ben's arm. There was a look of panic on the kid's face. "I want to go with you."

The old man, though, was as calm as ever. "Be patient, Luke. Stay and watch over the droids. They *must* be delivered safely, or other star systems will suffer the same fate as Alderaan. Your destiny lies along a different path than mine."

Han rolled his eyes so hard at Ben's dramatic tone they should have gone flying out of his head.

"The Force will be with you, always," Ben said. He pulled his hood up over his head, then felt for the lightsaber at his side. When the door opened, he ducked out into the long grey hall. Luke stood there a moment, watching him go, before shutting the door.

Han leaned over the console, checking on the *Falcon* below. The R2 droid started whistling like crazy, its head spinning back towards Luke.

"What is it?" Luke asked.

"Wait – slow down, Artoo! Sir, I'm afraid I'm not entirely sure. He says, 'I found her,' and keeps repeating, 'She's here, she's here.'"

"Who?" Luke asked before Han could.

"Why, Princess Leia, sir."

"The princess?" Luke cried. "She's here?"

Han blinked. "Princess? What's going on?"

"Indeed," Threepio said, interpreting Artoo's beeping for them. "Level five. Detention block AA twenty-three. I'm . . . I'm afraid she's scheduled to be terminated."

Han could have groaned. If anything was going to light an unwanted fire under Luke, a damsel in distress was. Still . . . the name sounded familiar. Princess Leia . . . Leia . . . Where had he heard that before?

"We've got to do something!" Luke said.

"What are you even talking about?" Han asked.

"The droid – Artoo – he belongs to her. She recorded a message for Ben to find, saying she needed his help delivering something stored on the droid to her father on Alderaan."

Yikes. Unless her father had left the planet before it was destroyed, no one was delivering anything to anyone.

"Now, look," Han began, "don't get any funny ideas. The old man wants us to wait right here."

It was like he hadn't spoken at all. Luke ignored him and turned back to the droids. "Can you find a way into the detention block?"

"I'm not going anywhere," Han said. He'd hang around long enough for the old man to disable the tractor beam, and then he was gone. With or without the kid.

No . . . that wasn't true. He wouldn't leave without the kid. Luke would get himself killed. An unwanted fear gripped Han's stomach, turning it over.

"They're going to *execute* her!" Luke said. "Look, a few minutes ago you said you didn't want to just wait here to be captured. Now all you want to do is stay."

Nice tactic, turning Han's words against him. Smooth, kid.

"Marching into the detention area is not what I had in mind. They'll execute us, too, if we're caught."

Something lit behind Luke's eyes, and when he looked at Han again, there was a small knowing smile on his face. "She's *rich*."

Chewbacca swivelled towards the kid, suddenly interested, and growled.

"Rich?" Han repeated slowly. "How rich are we talking?"

"Listen," Luke began. "If you were to rescue her, the reward would be . . ."

Han caught himself leaning forwards. "What?"

"Well, more wealth than you can imagine!" Luke finished.

"I don't know. I can imagine quite a bit!" Enough

to swim through, roll around in, and maybe buy himself his own personal island on a planet where Jabba could never find him.

"And you'll get it! All of it!"

Han leaned back against the console, crossing his arms over his chest as he considered that. Any amount he could dream up, huh? A reward of that magnitude would get Jabba off his back and set him up for – what, exactly? Going legal with his business? Buying some property and settling down? Chewie had a family to support, but what would Han even do with the money, other than put it back into the *Falcon* or buy a new ship?

The kid could dream all he wanted about being a big-shot hero, rescuing princesses, but Han was just a normal guy trying to keep his skin – and, if he could, rescue the dreamers from their delusions. Casting a worried look at Luke, Han tried to imagine a scenario where the kid would be able to make it out of the battle station without his help. Luke might have had the heart, but there were times you had to be heartless to survive.

But if Han were being honest . . . he would admit that it stung, just a little bit, that the kid assumed everything he did was for money.

"I'd better," he told Luke. "All of it."

Han looked at Chewie, waiting for his grunt of agreement. When he had it, he asked, "What's your plan?"

Luke glanced around, eyes catching on something on the console. "Threepio – can you hand me those binders?"

Holding the binders, he took a step closer to Chewie. "OK. Now I'm going to put these on you. . . ."

Chewie liked that idea about as much as he liked getting haircuts. He let out a furious roar, pride ruffled.

"Er, OK. Han, you put them on. . . ." Luke quickly shoved the binders into Han's hands.

"Don't worry, Chewie. I think I know what he has in mind. Easy, buddy. You know it's just pretend," Han assured him.

Still, his heart gave a little jerk over how worried

Chewie looked as Han snapped the electronic binders in place.

"Master Luke, sir!" Threepio said. "Pardon me for asking, but what should Artoo and I do if we're discovered here?"

Luke picked up his stormtrooper helmet again. "Lock the door!"

"And hope they don't have blasters," Han added.

CHAPTER TWELVE

THE MOMENT THE elevator doors slid open on the detention block, Han knew they were in trouble.

"This isn't going to work," he muttered.

"Why didn't you say so before?" Luke hissed back.

"I *did* say so before!" At least five times since they had left the control room. It wasn't Han's fault Luke heard only what he wanted to hear.

The detention block was everything Han didn't want it to be: well-protected by laser gates and cameras and well-manned by a half dozen security officers. One of those officers looked up from the processing station as Han, Luke and Chewie approached. His lip peeled back in disgust as he looked the Wookiee over.

"Where are you taking this . . . thing?"

Han held his breath, fighting to keep his temper in check.

"Prisoner transfer from block one-one-three-eight," Luke said. Han was proud of how smoothly the lie rolled off the kid's tongue. Maybe Han was rubbing off on him after all.

"I wasn't notified." The security officer's eyes narrowed. "I'll have to clear it."

Blast. Han cast another nervous look around, sizing up the room as the officer walked back to the console. They were two seconds away from having a hole shot right through their story. As Luke stepped forwards, Han subtly reached over and unfastened one of Chewie's binders with a shrug.

Chewbacca wasted no time. He threw his arms up with a roar that frightened even Han. The Wookiee yanked the blaster free from Han's hands and began to fire.

"Look out!" Han shouted. "He's loose!"

"He's going to pull us apart!" Luke cried, overdoing it *just* a bit.

The security officers gaped at them, confused. It was the opening Han and Luke needed to pull out their own blasters. Luke quickly caught on that while Han was aiming in Chewie's general direction, all his shots were going wide – hitting cameras, the laser gate controls and finally the guards themselves.

A silence fell over the detention block as the last of the security officers slumped forwards. Han's ears were ringing too loudly for him to hear the faint alarm chirping from the processing station. When he did, his pulse kicked up a notch.

He pulled off his helmet and rushed over to the console, scanning through the list of prisoners. "Here it is. . . . Your princess is in cell twenty-one eight-seven. Go get her – I'll hold them off."

Luke nodded, then scampered up the stairs to the long dark row of cells. Han took a deep breath and cleared his throat, his finger poised above the comlink. One of them must have grazed it with a shot because it was still sparking and smoking as he pushed the button to establish a connection.

"Everything is under control," he said in his best official, yes-I-belong-here voice. "Situation normal."

"What happened?" a voice crackled through the still-smoking intercom. Han jumped as a spark shot out of it.

"Uh . . . we had a slight weapons malfunction." His voice sounded painfully awkward to his own ears, so he could only imagine what the person on the other end was thinking. "But, um, everything's perfectly all right now. We're fine. We're all fine here, now, thank you. How are you?"

He cringed.

"We're sending a squad up," came the immediate response.

"Uh, um, negative, negative. We have a reactor leak here now. Give us a few minutes to lock it down. Large leak . . . very, uh, dangerous."

"Who is this? What's your operating number?"

Oh, well. Han leaned back, blasting out the comlink entirely. "Boring conversation anyway." He cupped his hands around his mouth and shouted down the hall. "Luke! We're going to have company!"

Chewie howled a question to him from where he stood by the door, blaster at the ready.

"I just jammed the doors," Han told him. "They won't be able to get in – "

There was a low, terrifying buzz from the other side of the thick metal doors.

"Get behind me! Get behind me!" Han shouted. The Wookiee scampered away, falling back closer to the cells. The rattle of explosions on the other side of the door shook Han down to his bones. He knew the moment they had broken through. The wave of heat that came off the door singed his skin.

Then the stormtroopers began to pour through the opening they'd made.

Han coughed against the smoke and fiery air as he and Chewie turned and ran up the hallway of cells. They nearly collided with Luke and – It wasn't often that Han found himself caught off guard. But standing in front of him, big brown eyes blazing, face bright from the short run she'd just taken, dark hair falling out of ridiculous coils around her ears, was one of the loveliest women Han had ever seen. That face – where had he seen that face?

"Can't get out that way," he managed, when he remembered they were in danger of being fried into little crispy versions of themselves.

The princess's gaze sharpened. "Looks like you managed to cut off our only escape route."

Her tone was designed to cut and did. The soft-focus dreams in his head evaporated. He turned back to the approaching stormtroopers and fired off another shot. "Maybe you'd like it back in your cell, Your Highness?"

Luke pulled Han and the princess into an alcove behind him. He tugged the comlink transmitter off his utility belt, trying to talk and fire at the same time. "See-Threepio! See-Threepio!"

"Yes, sir?" The droid was barely audible over the comlink.

"We've been cut off! Are there any other ways out of the detention block? . . . What was that? I didn't copy!"

If the droid responded, Han didn't hear it. His entire focus was on the seemingly endless stream of stormtroopers pushing through the hole in the doors. Chewie fell back even closer to Han, casting a worried look in his direction. If they didn't get going soon, they were going to become permanent residents.

Chewie yelped as a laser shot came within millimetres of taking off his nose.

"There isn't any other way out!" Luke called.

Of course. *Of course.* "I can't hold them off forever!" Han yelled. "Now what?"

"This is some rescue," the princess said. "When you came in here, didn't you have a plan for getting out?"

Han jerked a thumb back towards Luke. "He's the brains, sweetheart."

Luke, at least, looked a little sheepish. "Well, I didn't – "

Without missing a beat, the princess ripped the blaster rifle out of the kid's hands and spun towards Han. With startling accuracy, she shot out a grate just behind him, sending the scorched metal flying.

"What are you *doing*?" Han cried.

"Somebody has to save our skins!" she shouted, fire in her eyes. She gestured towards the hole she'd created. "Into the garbage chute, fly boy!"

Huh. Once again, Han found himself mostly speechless. He had expected tears. Grateful kisses, maybe. Not a tiny wisp of a girl with the bite of an acklay. She must have had Vader cowering in fear.

The princess fired a shot as she crossed from one side of the hall to the other. She tossed the gun back to Luke and dove into the chute. Chewbacca dropped back with a pitiful whine after taking a deep whiff of the opening.

"Get in there, you big furry oaf! I don't care what you smell!"

Han gave him a kick, sending his copilot through the tiny hole. Luke ducked to his side of the hall, backing Han up with his rifle. The kid seemed a bit too excited to be seeing – if Han had to guess – his first real firefight.

"Wonderful girl!" Han told him. "Either I'm going to kill her or I'm beginning to like her. Get in there!"

Luke threw him an exasperated look but jumped into the darkness of the opening. Han fired off a few more quick shots to create a cover of smoke, then dove headfirst down the chute – Right into some of the foulest muck and garbage the galaxy had ever seen. Clumps of half-rotted garbage swirled with the waste that was being pumped in from the bathrooms. Sticky flecks of blackened fruit and unidentifiable food clung to battered crates and scrap metal. Han gagged as he came up for air, grateful he'd kept his mouth closed as he came down. There was a single light overhead, illuminating just how little there was to see. Chewie had found a small platform leading to a hatch but was clearly struggling to get it open. The sound of Luke sloshing around, up to his waist in crud, bounced off the impossibly high walls.

"Here, Leia," Luke said. "Let me help you."

Leia, huh? Not *Princess* or *Your Highness*? Look at the kid, already on a first-name basis with royalty. Too bad she didn't want his help as she climbed up onto some kind of overturned crate. The darkness and damp air made Han feel like they'd landed right in a swamp.

"The garbage chute was a wonderful idea. What an incredible smell you've discovered!" Han said sarcastically. "Let's get out of here. Move, Chewie."

"No!" Luke shouted. "Wait!"

But Han had already raised his gun and fired at the hatch. He watched in horror as the bolt bounced off the metal and ricocheted around the compartment. The princess and Luke both dove for cover in the garbage and Chewie howled in outrage.

"I already tried it!" Luke said. "It's magnetically sealed."

The princess rounded on Han, furious. She looked like she wanted to strangle him. "Put that thing away! You're going to get us all killed!"

Han gave a mocking salute. "Look, I had everything under control until you led us down here.

You know, it's not going to take them long to figure out what happened to us."

The girl had the nerve to stick her chin up, looking down her nose at him. "It could be worse."

As soon as the words were out of her mouth, an inhuman moan bellowed through the small chamber. Chewie threw himself against the hatch, actually cowering.

"Surprise!" Han said. "It's worse!"

She glared at him.

He glared at her.

Han was vaguely aware of Luke's saying, "I think there's something alive in here!" before Han rounded on the princess and muttered, "Still waiting on that 'Thank you for rescuing me from my imminent execution.' You might be a princess but you've got less manners than I do!"

If Han had been standing even one centimeter closer to her, he had no doubt the smirk would have been slapped clear off his face.

"How *dare* you!" Leia said, her voice strained – not just with anger but with some other emotion that sounded suspiciously like pain. "I'm a senator – I *was* a senator!"

Even in her anger, real grief shadowed her eyes. The sight momentarily brought Han up short. They'd all had a bad day, but hers had clearly been the worst of all.

"I think something just moved past my leg . . ." Luke said, climbing over a floating pole somewhere behind Han.

"Congratulations, Your Worshipfulness," Han said finally. "Do you expect me to kiss your hand? Or will a bow and a little grovelling suffice?"

"Look – did you see that?" Luke might have pointed at something, but Han waved him off, his whole attention focused on the little thermal detonator in a white dress, steaming and spitting at him like she was about to go off.

"Like you know anything about manners, you overgrown ape!"

"Guys – seriously – "

The anxiety in Luke's voice made Han turn towards him.

"It's your imagination, kid – "

Luke let out a hoarse cry as he was violently yanked down into the waste and muck, disappearing from sight.

CHAPTER THIRTEEN

---⚓---

HAN STARED AT the ripple in the slime-coated water where Luke had been standing no more than a second before. Disbelief held him hostage for a moment, and then, to his surprise, it was fear that exploded out of him. Not only because letting Luke die would probably void his deal with Ben but because no one, especially not an innocent kid, deserved to drown under scummy Imperial garbage.

Han scrambled towards the spot where the kid had gone under. "Luke! *Luke!*"

Blast it all – he couldn't have lost the kid, not already, not yet, not ever.

"*Luke!*" Leia screamed, digging under the garbage.

The disgusting water sprayed up around them

as Luke broke through the surface. A slimy green tentacle was wrapped around his neck, keeping him in a stranglehold.

"Grab on!" Leia said, extending a long silver pole towards him.

"*Shoot it!*" Luke gasped out. "My gun's jammed – "

"Where?" Han said, trying to aim.

"*Anywhere!*" Luke screamed, then was pulled under again.

Han shot down into the muck, hoping against hope he wasn't about to hit the kid's leg. He should have tried grabbing for Luke instead, because once he caught sight of the creature's single bulbous red eye with a slit pupil, he knew exactly what they were dealing with: a dianoga. Trash monster. Garbage squid. They infested city sewers, scavenging for food with their tentacles, and once they found a meal they wouldn't give it up without a fight. He didn't even want to guess how one had ended up on a battle station.

"*Luke!*" Han shouted, frantically trying to aim. He was a good shot, but he was shooting blind!

A metallic clang boomed through his ears, so hard the chamber seemed to shake with it. Han kept his focus on clearing the muck, trying to search for any sign of life. There was a beat of silence, and then Luke launched himself up through the water again, gasping and coughing.

"Grab him!" Leia called, scrambling over to them. "What happened?"

"I don't know!" Luke said, still gagging. "It just let go of me all of a sudden!"

And there it was again, that dread creeping over Han.

"I've got a bad feeling about this," he told the others. His new life motto, apparently. No Force necessary to know for certain.

And because he had the worst luck of any life form in the galaxy, two of the opposing walls rumbled and began to push inward. Han's eyes went wide. They were in a trash compactor, and if they didn't get out in the next few minutes, they would be flattened.

"Don't just stand there!" Leia barked. "Try

to brace the walls with something."

She was struggling under the weight of a metal beam, trying to wedge it between the walls pressing closer, closer, closer. Han grabbed one end of the beam, helping her get it into place. The force of the walls bent the thick metal like it was made of plastic.

"Threepio!" Luke was calling into his comlink. "Threepio! Come in, Threepio! Where could he be?"

This was bad, bad, bad, *bad*. Chewie jumped down off the platform to help them, but there was nothing strong enough down there to stop the walls. The princess had a sharp tongue, but she was practically pocket-sized compared with the Wookiee. And the more garbage that got pushed towards them, the higher it piled up, threatening to crush her.

Han pointed to a stack of crates and bins. "Get to the top!"

"I can't!" Leia said. Her composure had shattered, and panic was creeping in. Han was rattled by the sight of it, and when he tried reaching out to steady her, he slipped and went crashing down into the soggy muck.

"Threepio!" Luke was still yelling. "Threepio, will you come in?"

The walls were close enough now that Han manoeuvred so his back was against one side and his feet were pressed against the other. Leia tried to follow suit, but the sopping wet dress tangled around her legs made it almost impossible for her to pull herself up. Her swearing scorched even *his* ears.

"Easy, easy," he told her when he felt her starting to panic again. His arms strained as he reached down and helped her clamber up next to him. No matter how hard Han braced himself and pushed his legs out, it was like trying to hold back a Star Destroyer. Leia reached out blindly with her hand, and Han seized it. Hey, if he was going to die, at least it would be next to a beautiful girl.

"Well, one thing's for sure," Han said as his legs were pushed up closer to his chest. "We're all going to be a lot thinner!"

"Are you there, sir?" C-3PO's voice crackled through the comlink so suddenly, Han was afraid Luke would drop it.

"Shut down all the garbage mashers on the detention level!" Luke yelled into the comm. "Do you copy?"

It was too late for that. As they pushed together, the walls piled the trash and waste up and up and up until Han could no longer see the ceiling. Metal beams and crates snapped and crumbled, falling onto their heads. He scrambled to keep both himself and the princess climbing, but where could they go? There wasn't any way out.

"Pardon me?" the droid sounded confused.

Were the walls moving even faster now? Han braced his back against one wall and walked his feet up the other, willing to try anything to keep them alive even a second longer. It was getting harder to breathe. Small scraps of plastic slipped into the joints of his stormtrooper armour, stabbing into his back and neck.

Han had always expected to go down with his

ship. Blown to bits in one last burst of glory. Turning into a mashed puddle of goo was *not* part of the plan. He looked around, searching for something, anything, to brace the walls.

"Threepio!" Luke shouted. "Shut down all the garbage mashers on the detention level!"

Han struggled to pull himself up that tiny bit more, trying to see if Luke was still OK. The whole room shuddered like a quake, but he was so focused on looking for the kid, he initially missed the fact that the walls had stopped moving. The four of them looked at one another, holding their breaths in disbelief. Then Han let out a loud, overjoyed holler that Luke echoed back. Chewie practically crushed the kid in his excited grip, and even the princess let her guard down enough to throw her arms around Han's neck.

"Curse my metal body! I wasn't fast enough. It's all my fault! My poor master!" The droid's voice was still pouring out of the comlink. He was clearly distressed and hearing their cheers as screams.

"Threepio, we're all right," Luke said, laughing.

"You did great. Can you open the pressure maintenance hatch on unit number . . . where are we?" He looked around for some kind of label.

"Three-two-six-three-eight-two-seven," Han said, pointing to the muck-splattered numbers above the hatch.

The click of the hatch depressurising and opening was one of the sweetest sounds Han had ever heard. He and the others scrambled out into an empty hall. Glancing around as he stripped off the filthy stormtrooper armour, Han took in the plastic sheets and construction signs around them. Good. This section would be deserted.

"If we can just avoid any more of the princess's bright ideas, we ought to be able to get out of here," he said.

And just like that, the relief on her face was replaced with a look of utter disdain. "I don't know who you are or where you come from, but from now on you do as I tell you. OK?"

Han wanted to scoff and brush off her words, but, truthfully, the intense way she glared at him was a little scary. Luke hadn't rescued himself a delicate little bloom.

"Look, Your Worshipfulness, let's get one thing straight. I take orders from one person." He pointed at his chest. *"Me."*

"It's a wonder you're still alive!" Leia spun on her heel, nearly colliding with Chewie. "Will someone get this big walking carpet out of my way?"

Han shot an accusatory look at Luke as she stormed ahead of them. "No reward is worth this."

Luke sighed. "Come on."

They rushed through the empty hallway, and Han was surprised to see that, when it intersected with another long sleek corridor, he knew where they were.

"This way," he said, taking them in the opposite direction the princess wanted to head in. She grumbled something under her breath but followed until they reached a large bay window. Below them, right where they had left her, was the *Millennium Falcon.* And, boy, she'd never looked more beautiful. Even surrounded by a dozen stormtroopers.

"Threepio, do you copy?" Luke said into his comlink.

"For the moment," the droid said. "We've moved to the main hangar across from the ship."

"We're right above you. Stand by."

Leia stepped up next to Han, casting a cool look over the ship. "You came in that thing? You're braver than I thought."

"Nice." Han shot her a dirty look. "Come on."

He jogged down the hall at the head of the group, rounding the next corner to where he thought the elevators should be – and right into a squad of eight stormtroopers.

"It's them!" one of the troopers shouted. "Blast them!"

Without sparing a single thought to how spectacularly stupid the idea was, Han charged forwards, firing wildly into the squad and shouting as he went. Despite the odds, the stormtroopers turned and fled, but Han didn't stop. Chewie roared after him, his heavy steps pounding the ground behind Han. These were the people who'd imprisoned

Han, his ship, and his best friend on this death trap. These were the people who were ruining his one real shot at getting Jabba off his back and taking control of his life again. His anger pushed him forwards like a wave, heating the blood in his veins. Let them *try* to keep him. Let them *try* to hold his *Falcon*. To execute the princess, hurt the kid – Wait, no – the kid and the princess had *nothing* to do with it. Right. This attack was about the *Falcon*. If it also *happened* to give Luke and Leia an opening to get down to the hangar, then great, but it was revenge, pure and simple. His heart thundering, Han fired his blaster wildly, shouting louder, drowning out every thought in his head.

Unfortunately, his courage flamed out the second he reached the end of the hallway, which just so happened to lead into a hangar full of stormtroopers. Han's boots skidded as he tried to stop himself from crashing into them. Blood draining from his face, he whirled around and started running in the opposite direction as laser bolts chased him back down the hall. Chewie came into view up ahead, clearly confused.

"Let's go, let's go!" Han cried, tugging his copilot towards a nearby door – stairs! It felt like they took the steps three at time, flying down them until they reached the lower level. Han held up a hand, signalling to Chewie to wait as he stuck his head out of the door at the base of the stairs.

The hangar. It was still crawling with stormtroopers, but they'd made it that far. Han pulled the Wookiee over to a stack of crates and ducked down, keeping an eye out for Leia and Luke.

Chewie rumbled out a question, reaching over to smack the back of Han's head.

"I'll admit, I could have used a plan just then," Han whispered. "But it turned out fine, right?"

The longer he stared at his ship, her grey metallic plates gleaming under the harsh hangar lights, the more restless Han felt. What was taking the kid so long? And where was the fossil? Every second they wasted was another missed opportunity to escape.

"We could go," Han said slowly. "Just you and

me. It'll be a risk, especially if the old man hasn't disabled the tractor beam . . . but we could find another job."

The Wookiee shook his head, sadness crystallising in his eyes. Han felt his friend's disappointment as surely as if Chewie had reached over and smacked him again.

Chewbacca's next words hit Han like a punch to the chest. *It's OK to care about them. They need our help.*

Han had never let himself get tied too closely to causes. He was fine with the Rebellion so long as it created more business for him and fine with the Empire so long as it kept *out* of his business.

"I care about them," Han said. "We don't get paid if we bring back bodies."

But even as he said it, he was surprised to find the words ringing false in his own ears – to feel an uncomfortable twinge in his chest. Remembering that moment of white-hot fear when the dianoga had pulled Luke under, and how terror had cracked the princess's tough armour when she thought they'd be crushed, Han couldn't help but acknowledge the quiet feeling that had been sneaking up on him.

He *did* care.

They say battle can form unbreakable bonds between soldiers, but Han realised it wasn't the fighting itself; it was that they had worked together, that they'd made it through to the other side. In a few hours, he'd come to understand Luke better than he did some of his smuggling buddies he'd known for years.

Chewie growled another question, all innocence. He stroked a hand down over Han's head, but the smuggler brushed it off.

"No!" he whispered, pointing at the Wookiee. "Dump that thought right now. We aren't going to join up and get ourselves killed for nothing."

Join the Rebellion? It wasn't so much the idea of the fight that had Han's head pounding. What Chewie was talking about was investing in a cause, making a commitment for their future. Being tied to some idea.

Chewie crossed his arms over his chest. *You're better than this*, he said.

"You really think so?" Han asked. Sometimes he didn't feel better than that. Sometimes he felt like the biggest coward on that side of the galaxy.

"You're right," he admitted. "I wouldn't have left them."

Han had been called a lot of things in his life – scum, scoundrel, smuggler – but he wasn't heartless. Chewie's rumbling reply brought a faint smile to his lips. "I like the kid, too. But unless he wants to come with us, we're splitting with both him and the princess after this. We have to get Jabba off our backs. Otherwise there is no future for us."

A new burst of blaster fire announced Luke and Leia's arrival in the hangar. Han jumped to his feet and ran towards them.

"Get to the ship!" he cried, trying to take out at least a few of the stormtroopers on his way. Out of the corner of his eye, he caught the hangar's floodlights glinting off the droids' metallic skin. They scurried forwards, towards the *Falcon*'s ramp.

"Luke, let's go!" Han shouted, tugging at the kid's arm. Luke's feet were fixed to the ground, something like shock pouring over his face. He turned to look where Luke pointed to another set of open blast doors.

Two figures – one as black and shiny as a smear of oil, the other hooded in a thick brown cloak – circled each other. Their lightsabers vibrated in their hands, as different from each other as their owners were. One was sky blue, the other crimson – like burning blood.

So that was Darth Vader, huh? Always terrifying to realise rumours weren't exaggerated. The man – creature – *thing* was a giant, towering over the old man. His armour looked thick enough to keep him alive even in the freezing vacuum of space. The lights on his chest panel flickered, the way a droid's would.

The swords hissed and sizzled as they clashed; Ben and Darth Vader danced around each other like seasoned fighters, lost in their own world. Han realised he was staring as hard as the kid and tried again to tug him back towards the ship. The stormtroopers who had chased Luke and Leia into the hangar had turned their attention to the swordfight.

Ben looked over, the troopers' approach catching his attention. Then he looked past them. To where Luke was standing, dumbstruck. To Han. Han couldn't be sure – the old man was just too far away – but he thought Ben might have given him a nod just before he turned back to face Darth Vader. Ben drew his blade in and made no effort to stop Vader's lightsaber from slashing through him.

But instead of his body falling to pieces, an empty cloak fell to the ground. It was like the old man had just . . . disappeared. One last magic trick.

Han shook his head, the hair on the back of his neck rising. Maybe not magic at all.

"No!" Luke yelled. Han hooked an arm across the kid's chest and started to drag him away. For a second, he really thought the kid might make a

run for Vader. Luke's anger and disbelief rolled off him.

"Luke, we have to get out of here!" Leia shouted from the bottom of the ramp. The stormtroopers opened fire on her, forcing her to duck and run into the safety of the ship. Luke spun around one last time and fired a shot – not at Darth Vader but at the controls to the blast doors. They slammed shut just as Vader and the stormtroopers began to charge towards them.

"We have to go, kid," Han told him. "Before they fix the tractor beam!"

That snapped Luke out of his daze long enough for them to board the *Falcon*. Han raced towards the cockpit, where Chewie was already revving up the engine. He didn't realise Luke hadn't followed him in until he looked back over his shoulder, through the door, and saw the princess comforting him.

Han punched the controls, and they had hit open space before he took his next breath.

"All right, Chewie," he said as TIE fighters roared towards them in the distance. Only four.

He reached up, stroking his ship affectionately. She might have taken a knocking, but she would never let him down when it counted. "We're coming up on the sentry ships. Hold 'em off as long as you can. Angle the deflector shields while I charge up the main guns!"

Chewie roared his agreement, reaching up to flip through the switches. Han left his seat so fast it spun behind him.

For the longest time, if anyone asked Han why he was travelling alone, he'd give them the same line: *The name says it all — Solo.* And then he'd met Chewie, and suddenly that didn't apply anymore. The Wookiee knew, even if Han couldn't admit it to himself, that what scared Han wasn't putting his heart into a cause that would fail; it was losing the individuals he opened his heart to.

He wasn't free, not yet, not until he dealt with Jabba and repaid his debt. Even after, he'd never be like Luke. He wasn't meant to be a hero. But Han was beginning to suspect that he wasn't meant to be just a petty smuggler, either. The new friends he'd made had shown him that much. The old man would laugh if he knew Han was thinking it, but it was some strange stroke of luck – *destiny*, Ben would say – that had brought their little group together.

He ran towards the central hold to rally Luke to head to the gun ports, already imagining the weight of the ship's large blaster as it swung around and he took aim. Han knew losing themselves in another fight would be the best way for both him and the kid to burn off the sting of being forced to stand by helplessly as Ben was cut down.

The old man had sacrificed himself to save them. And it had taken seeing that for Han to question what would have happened if their situations had been reversed and he'd been the one in the position to make a sacrifice. Would he have done it? He wanted to believe that, yes, he would have. The thought made his chest feel tight. How incredible that, of all people, it was the old man who'd upended his universe, made him see the truth about himself with one selfless act of courage.

Han wasn't the best guy in the galaxy or the

smartest or even the most honest, and he wasn't sure he knew what he had done to deserve these friends.

But for now it was enough he wasn't flying solo anymore.

THE
FARM BOY

CHAPTER FOURTEEN

⚛

"I CAN'T BELIEVE HE'S GONE."

Those were the only words running through Luke's head, caught in some horrible loop, as the ship lurched into space. *I can't believe he's gone.* He slumped onto the bench by the game board on the *Millennium Falcon*, his legs finally giving out under him. Luke couldn't bring himself to move. He couldn't close his eyes, either, not without seeing the way Ben had looked just before . . .

He's dead, Luke thought. *Why can't I say it?*

Why did he have to keep seeing the way Ben had deactivated his lightsaber and hadn't tried to stop him – *Darth Vader.* The name hissed through Luke's mind like smoke, making the hairs on the backs of his arms rise. Just *seeing* the man . . . the *thing* had been enough to make Luke feel as if he were drenched in ice. The shock had left Luke useless as a droid with its circuits fried.

That was after Ben had told him that Vader had killed his father.

Vader had now taken another person from him.

Luke gripped the edge of the game board so hard he was sure the surface would crack. There was no one – nothing – in the galaxy he hated more than Darth Vader. He felt himself begin to shake, tears again threatening to spill over. Luke stubbornly scrubbed at his face. What good would crying do?

Even as the fury poured through him, its flames were doused by poisonous fear every time he pictured the stark lines of the monster's mask. What had Ben called him? That's right – a Sith. One who relied on the dark side of the Force instead of embracing the light.

Ben had promised that the Force had a plan for everything, that it guided their course through life. But how could the Force have let that happen? Why did evil have to win and win and win again? Luke knew he was supposed to trust in it, but, mostly, all he felt was hopeless.

Vader had beaten *Ben* – a legendary warrior, a Jedi Master. What would happen if Luke ever came face to face with the Sith? If he hunted Luke down, looking for the droids, looking for the princess? Luke had had a few hours of training; Ben had had *decades*! And still Vader had cut the Jedi Master down with a single blow. Leaving . . . nothing.

Because, as impossible as it seemed, at the moment the black-armoured warrior had sliced his crimson lightsaber through Ben, the Jedi Master had disappeared. Vanished.

Why?

And . . . Luke shook his head. He had to have imagined it. But he could have sworn that in the second after he felt his heart stop and before Han had grabbed him, he had heard Ben's voice inside his mind. *Run, Luke! Run!*

But that was insane, wasn't it? That kind of thing just didn't happen. Ben would have been speaking to him as . . . a spirit?

The shiver that crawled over his skin was chased away by the poncho someone draped over his shoulders right then. Luke looked up from where he'd rested his face against his arms to find Leia watching him.

The person he saw was an entirely different Leia from the haughty princess who'd taken one look at him after he'd opened her cell and said, "Aren't you a little short for a stormtrooper?" She was a different Leia from the one who'd blasted out the garbage chute and the one who'd thrown her arms around him in relief when they'd gotten out. He liked that about her. She wasn't at all what he had expected; he was a little ashamed, actually, to admit that he'd really thought the princess would swoon in relief at the sight of him coming to save her. She'd rescued them from her own rescue.

Luke heaved out a sigh, gratefully accepting the poncho. He wanted to say something, even just thank you, but every word seemed to catch in his throat.

"There wasn't anything you could have done.

Still, I'm so sorry," she said, kneeling down next to him. "That was General Kenobi, wasn't it? From what my father told me of him, he was a great man."

Luke nodded, a numbness settling in at his centre. He'd known Ben for only a day, and yet even he'd been able to see that Ben was a great man. But there was still so much about the Jedi he didn't know. And he hadn't actually given Luke any details about his life, not really. Something about that made Luke feel betrayed, and it brought his anger back up to a simmer beneath his skin.

I followed you, Luke thought, surprised at the flash of rage that sliced through him. *I lost everything and followed you. You promised that you'd teach me, Ben!* And now . . . what? How would he teach himself? The lightsaber clipped to his belt felt cold and heavy. Guilt and fear sat in his stomach, knocking its contents around, making him feel sick.

You must learn to control your emotions, otherwise they will control you. Ben had told him that when Luke was training with his lightsaber. All these things he was feeling now were tied to the dark side of the

Force. Luke hadn't understood at the time how that was possible, but now he saw how easy it would be to sink into his own helpless fury. To get lost and never come out of it.

"Blast it. What am I doing?" Luke said, sitting up. "You just lost your whole planet – "

"Loss is still loss," Leia said, her voice tight. She glanced away. "We just can't let it beat us. We have things to do."

"How are you so . . . OK?" he asked. "I feel like – in the past day, I've lost my only family, and now Ben. I've never been off my home world before, and now I'm a million kilometres away from it. It's like I've been knocked out of orbit and I don't know how to get right side up again. How do you do it?"

A wave of pain crossed Leia's face. She bit her lip, drawing in a deep breath. "I want to cry," she admitted, "all the time, every moment. But I know that if I start I won't be able to stop, and that's not useful right now. Our situations aren't the same, but I do know what you're feeling right now. What it's like to feel alone – "

"Even though you're surrounded by strangers?" Luke finished for her.

"Exactly!" Leia said, squeezing his arm. The expression on her face was still so heartbroken, Luke wanted to do something, anything, to make her feel better. But even he knew that was impossible. She *did* understand, and so did he.

"You were the one who found the droids, right?"

Luke looked up at the sudden question. "Yeah. We bought them off Jawas – these desert scavengers – to work on my uncle's farm. I found your message on the little guy while I was trying to clean him."

"And you went off to find General Kenobi because of it?" Leia asked.

"Well . . ." Luke rubbed the back of his neck, still a little embarrassed about being outsmarted by an astromech droid. "Artoo ran away to find him. Threepio and I found him, and then Ben found us just as we were being attacked by Sand People. Saved us all. While I was gone, stormtroopers came to the farm looking for the droids and . . . killed

Uncle Owen and Aunt Beru when they didn't find them."

Leia pulled back, looking stricken. "Luke – I can't even begin to tell you how sorry I am – all of this, it's all because of me. I was so desperate to get the plans to General Kenobi, I wasn't even thinking – "

"No, Leia," Luke said, resting his hands on her shoulders. "The only people responsible for my family and Ben's deaths are the Empire. *Vader.* I wish it didn't have to happen the way it did, but they didn't die for nothing. Getting the information you found to the Rebellion is all that matters now."

Leia looked down, rolling her shoulders back as she took in another, steadying breath. "Can I ask you something?"

"Yeah, of course."

She smoothed out the wrinkles in the fabric of her dress, running her fingers along the watery lines of the new stains. "Why did you rescue me?"

"Why wouldn't I have?" Luke asked, confused.

Was he just supposed to leave her there for the Empire to execute?

"You could have left once the tractor beam was disabled. I'm sure that's the plan our friend the captain was pulling for. You didn't have to risk being caught. General Kenobi could have brought the information to the Rebellion."

Luke was almost offended that she would think he was capable of just walking away. "Because you needed help. That's why. You don't need a reason to help people."

Leia looked up at that, and Luke saw a flicker of something in her eyes. Her face seemed alive with colour again. "You asked before, about how I hold it together?"

Luke nodded. He needed . . . some way to keep going without constantly falling back on his anger. He couldn't disrespect Ben's memory by ignoring what the Jedi had tried to teach him. He needed a way out of his cycle of hatred, and Leia seemed to have found one.

"I think about when I was very young, running

wild through the palace, playing hide-and-seek with my mother and father." She let out a faint laugh, smiling at the memory. "They were both so busy and important – they had the weight of the universe on their shoulders – but they still had this great huge capacity for fun and love. And *hope*. They never gave up on the idea that the galaxy could be a safe, beautiful place for all life. Joining the Rebellion finally let me have a real voice – a real way to fight for the changes I believed in. Now, fighting alongside them will be my way of honouring my parents and my people. It gives me a reason to push through and keep going. And . . . maybe it'll be the same for you."

Luke had run through such a range of emotions over the previous few days – horror at the loss of his family, the exhilaration of finally flying in space, the frustration of training, the terror of being shot at and trying to outrun and outgun the Empire . . . but at Leia's words, he felt something new: hope.

"Yeah," he said slowly. "I think I'd like that."

And when Leia offered him a tentative smile, he was finally able to return it.

At that moment, Han burst into the central hold area, face flushed and hair wild.

"Come on, buddy," he said. "We're not out of this yet! I need your help. You keep saying you can fly and shoot. Well, now's the time to prove it."

Luke was exhausted, wrung out by the day, but *that* sounded right up his alley. He passed the poncho back to Leia with a grateful look and said to Han, "Show me where."

Han grinned, slapping Luke's back. Luke followed him through the ship at a run, to a ladder well at the centre of the ship. At each end of the ladder was a gun port.

"Just aim and fire – and try to keep up with me, if you can!"

A trill of excitement finally found its way into Luke as he slid down the ladder. He'd seen from the outside of the ship that there were two long gun turrets – one on the top of the ship, the other below. "We'll see about that. . . ."

Luke hopped up into the seat behind the gun and picked up the headset hooked over it.

"You in, kid?" Han's voice came through the headphones.

"Yeah, I read," Luke said. He relaxed, just a little bit, when he saw the actual controls. While he had a viewport window to look through, there was also a target screen. Dozens of red blips were swarming towards the green one that represented the *Falcon*. He seized control of the laser gun's handles and swung the heavy thing around on its stand. Still . . . this was going to be a lot different from shooting womp rats in Beggar's Canyon; even he knew that. But he wasn't about to let Han or the others down. Luke moved his thumbs over the firing buttons, ready.

"OK, stay sharp!" Han said.

Leia must have gone into the cockpit with Chewbacca, because her voice filtered into his ears next. "Here they come!"

He heard the TIE fighters before he saw them streak past the viewport like shooting stars. The sound was piercing, as if the ships' engines were screaming. *Ack!* Despite how calm he felt, Luke jumped at the sudden sound, his thumbs hitting the firing buttons. *Yikes.* He forced himself to stop choking the controls and take actual aim before beginning to fire again. The gun sprayed out a line of laser beams, chasing the ships across the sky and back again without a single hit.

The *Millennium Falcon* bucked like an angry dewback as it took the TIE fighters' fire. Luke was sure he smelled smoke but kept that bit of information to himself as another three Imperial ships appeared. When they hit the *Falcon* again, Luke was nearly thrown out of his seat.

"They're coming in too fast!" he said between gritted teeth. Sweat made his hair stick to his face, his tunic hug his back.

The sound of an explosion somewhere overhead and a cheer from Han was the only response Luke got. So he had hit one. Luke set his shoulders, focusing on the ships again. He wasn't going to let Han get all the glory.

"We've lost lateral controls," Leia reported.

"Don't worry, she'll hold together," Han said, but he forgot to mute himself when he added, under his breath, "You hear me, baby? Hold together."

Somehow, Luke felt himself relaxing into the fight. It wasn't all that different from the way he'd felt handling his lightsaber. His racing heart settled into a steady rhythm. *I'm doing this,* he thought – really *doing it.* He was anticipating which direction the gleaming black-and-silver TIE fighters would come from, their evasive manoeuvres, until, finally –

The explosion of fiery dust from the destroyed Imperial ship momentarily blinded Luke. The thrill of victory raced through him, lifting him higher than he had thought possible. He pumped a fist in the air. "I got him! I got him!"

"Great, kid!" Han said as he hit another TIE fighter, sending it spiraling into space like a smoking comet. "Don't get cocky!"

It didn't even bother Luke anymore that Han – who couldn't have been more than ten years older than Luke – would not stop calling him *kid.*

It had set Luke's teeth on edge the first few times, mostly because it had reinforced everything Luke had hated about his life on Tatooine. He had felt as if he were never going to grow up, never going to move on, as if he'd always be living out in the deep desert with his aunt and uncle and a group of friends at Anchorhead he wasn't totally sure even liked him – because, seriously, who gave someone they liked the nickname Wormie?

Luke had applied for the Imperial Academy a few months before, hoping that would be the year Uncle Owen stopped acting like Luke was crucial to running their little moisture farm and let him go. There were moments Luke had really believed he would never break through the sunset colours of Tatooine's atmosphere.

Now, the thought of it just made Luke grin. Because even as a *kid*, he and his best friend, Biggs, had flow through the craggy teeth of Beggar's Canyon in their T-16 skyhoppers. He'd clipped his ship's wings so many times, it was a wonder he was still alive. But he hadn't stopped, not until he could hit the most womp rats as the hairy, monstrous little pests scurried through the canyon ravines and washes. Not until he had the fastest time flying through.

This kid was more than happy to show the captain up – and do it in Ben's honour.

Luke destroyed the next two TIE fighters that had the misfortune of landing on his target screen.

I'm in space, he thought over and over again. *I'm doing it.* And still, even watching the Imperial ships blow apart, he couldn't believe it. He couldn't wrap his mind around how much his life had changed in *hours,* never mind days, weeks, years. Luke was shocked he didn't have whiplash.

"There are still two more of them out there," Leia said.

"On it!" Luke called.

"Not if I get there first!" Han sounded like he was having just as much fun as Luke was.

Swinging his chair around again, Luke kept his thumbs on the firing buttons. The gun vibrated his hands as he took careful aim at the TIE fighter trying to strike at the *Falcon* from below. With a deep breath, he turned the laser onto the Imperial ship and watched, practically jumping out of his seat in excitement when it blew apart.

The last enemy dot on the radar disappeared as Han took out the remaining TIE fighter. The *Falcon* rumbled with the aftershock of the final explosion.

And then they were all clear.

A relieved laugh burst out of Luke. "We did it! We did it!"

He stood up from the gun port so fast he was yanked back down by the cord of his headset. Untangling himself from the wire, he threw the headset down and climbed up the ladder just as Han was climbing down his. The smuggler clasped Luke's shoulder, grinning.

"Nice shooting, kid! They teach you that out on the moisture farm?"

Luke shook his head, his energy deflating. Han hadn't meant it as an insult – at least Luke didn't think he had – but the words still stung. He wasn't just some farm kid. He'd always wanted to be something more than that.

They passed by Chewbacca, who was busy fishing C-3PO out from where he'd fallen into a compartment that must have flown open. R2 beeped at Chewie's side, urging him on.

"It's terrible, isn't it? I'm maimed. . . ." Threepio's voice faded as they entered the cockpit.

"Not a bad bit of rescuing, huh?" Han said, throwing his gloves onto the nearest seat. Luke trailed behind him, taking in the sight of Leia standing up from the pilot's seat and moving to one of the two in the back. "Sometimes I even amaze myself."

Leia leveled a look of utter contempt at Han. "That doesn't sound too hard."

Luke's heart lightened a bit at that. At least he wouldn't have to compete with Han for Leia's attention. As Uncle Owen had once explained, some creatures were just natural enemies. He couldn't leave the two of them alone – not because he was afraid the smuggler would put the moves on Leia but because he was genuinely worried they would eventually try clawing each other's faces off.

"Besides," Leia continued, raising her chin. "They let us go. It's the only explanation for the ease of our escape."

"Easy?" Han repeated in disbelief as he slumped into the pilot's seat. "You call that *easy*?"

"They must be tracking us, hoping we lead them back to the Rebellion."

Luke's blood slowed in his veins at that. He hadn't even *considered* it as a possibility. Maybe he really was just a dumb farm kid in need of a good hard reality check.

"Not this ship, sister," Han said, lacing his hands behind his head, all confidence.

Luke could tell by the way she was struggling to control not only her expression but also her tone that Leia was frustrated. "At least the information in Artoo is safe," she said.

"What's so important? What's he carrying?" Han asked.

"The technical readouts of that battle station," she replied.

"What?" Luke said, almost leaping out of his seat in shock. He would never have let the R2 unit out of his sight if he'd known! He wasn't sure what he had thought the "information vital to the survival of the Rebellion" she mentioned in her message was, but – but it hadn't been *that*!

"I only hope that when the data is analysed, a weakness can be found in the battle station's defenses. There has to be a way to destroy it," Leia said. "We still have a chance. This isn't over yet!"

Han suddenly looked like a wild animal that had been backed into a corner. "It is for me. I ain't in this for your revolution, and I expect to be well paid for my trouble."

Luke knew that his new friend wasn't exactly noble and would never claim to be, but . . . really? Disappointment thundered through him. Luke shook his head. After all that, it still boiled down to money? He couldn't have misread the guy *that* badly . . . could he?

"I have my own problems to deal with," Han muttered, looking back out towards the stars.

Leia had been caught off guard by his response, and if Luke had thought she was angry before, it was nothing compared with now. Her voice was colder than the freezing vacuum of space. "You needn't worry about your reward. If money is all that you love, then that's what you'll receive!"

That was the problem, wasn't it? Luke knew Han loved his credits, but that wasn't all he loved. Luke had seen real *good* in him. Or, uh, at least the potential for good when he wasn't distracted by thoughts of his bank account.

Han's smirk slipped, just for a second, as Leia turned and started towards the cockpit door.

"Your friend is quite a mercenary," she said to Luke, loudly enough to ensure that Han would hear. "I wonder if he really cares about anything . . . or anyone."

"*I* care," Luke called after her lamely.

"Smooth, kid," Han said with a chuckle.

Luke flushed as he took Chewbacca's empty copilot chair. He could count the number of girls his age he'd known on Tatooine with one hand,

and all of them had been taken. It was hard enough to figure out what to say to a girl without her also being one of the most impressive people in the entire galaxy.

Luke asked, trying to sound casual, "What do you think of her?"

Han raised an eyebrow. "I'm trying not to, kid."

"Good," Luke muttered under his breath.

"Still . . . she's got a lot of spirit," Han said. "I don't know, do you think a princess and a guy like me . . . ?"

"*No.*"

Luke realised his mistake when he looked up from under his bangs and saw the teasing smile on Han's face. The smuggler was still laughing as he pushed the lever in front of him forwards, sending the ship hurtling into hyperspace.

CHAPTER FIFTEEN

T HE FOURTH MOON orbiting the planet Yavin was like something out of one of the storybooks Aunt Beru used to read to him. Back then, he'd been no taller than R2 and, having seen nothing past the shimmering dunes outside his window, couldn't imagine what a tree looked like. His aunt had a soft, kind heart compared with Uncle Owen's, which had been roughened and sandblasted by years of disappointments. One day, when Uncle Owen had business in Mos Eisley, his aunt had taken him into Anchorhead, the nearest outpost town, to use the holonet connection there. She'd brought up images of forests and rivers and oceans for him to marvel at. The three-dimensional pictures had floated in the space in front of him, but they hadn't felt real; he hadn't been able to touch or smell them.

His heart went painfully tight in his chest at the thought of his aunt and uncle. Every time Luke closed his eyes, he could see what the stormtroopers had done to his family, to their homestead, when they had come looking for the droids. He honestly believed what he'd told Leia; he hadn't said it to make her feel better or to ease her guilt, knowing she was suffering from loss, too. He would always believe that the only people to blame were the soldiers of the Empire.

But Luke was sure he'd never forget the sickening feeling of dread that had overwhelmed him as he'd raced home from Ben's in his landspeeder. Some part of him had known he was too late, but he'd kept hoping. *Just let me get there in time. Let it be someone else's farm. Let them be OK. . . .* The monstrous cloud of smoke billowing from the burned-out shell of his home had been visible from kilometres away, a black beacon against the sky. Too late. Luke hated those words. *Too late.* There'd been nothing left to do but bury the people who had raised him.

Leia glanced over at him, as if sensing his thoughts. Without a word, she slid her hand into his and gave it a quick, tight squeeze. The small gesture was reassuring but didn't settle his mind or help him break the cycle of his thoughts.

In the rare moments when he wasn't wishing he had been home, that he could have protected his family, he remembered what Ben had said – that he would have been killed, too. That didn't ease the throbbing hurt in his chest, but it did make him more determined than ever to make the most of his chance to destroy the Empire and everything it represented. First, though, the Rebellion would have to accept him. And that . . . wasn't exactly guaranteed.

The *Falcon* swept down through the soft, feathery clouds as they parted to reveal endless kilometres of thick rich green. It was a shade Luke had never seen in his life, not even in clothes. The trees were so thick and packed together that Luke couldn't see through their leaves to the ground.

For one horrible, embarrassing moment, Luke couldn't think of the word to describe it. Then Han came to his rescue.

"Jungle," Han groaned. "Hope everyone packed their bug spray."

"There." Leia leaned between Chewbacca and Han, pointing to a silver lookout post and the uniformed soldier keeping guard there. "They'll be in the temples just beyond that. . . . See?"

They were so focused on the towering dark stone pyramids that had just come into view, they missed the streak of red that shot out of a gun hidden in the trees. Everyone but Han was tossed out of his or her seat. Luke hauled himself up, spinning back towards the viewport. They were actually firing at the *Falcon*? So much for smooth introductions!

"Nice friends you've got, Your Worshipfulness!" Han huffed, reaching for his comlink. Leia beat him to it, adjusting the frequency until she found the one she was looking for.

"This is . . ." Leia paused, a look of deep sadness coming over her features. Luke leaned forwards and briefly put a hand on her shoulder, but he was confused by her expression. She struggled to find the words. "Leia Organa. Authorization code delta-alpha-nu-five-five. Requesting permission to land."

There was a split second of silence that made Luke's hands tighten around his seat's armrests. Then shouts of joy exploded from the radio, the sound too loud and messy to pick apart what any one of them was trying to say. Their growing excitement registered like a buzz in Luke's ears.

"Granted." The voice that responded was deep, grave. "Use the landing pad near the eastern temple. We'll tow you into the hangar."

"No need," Han said loudly. "We ain't staying."

Really? Luke thought, rubbing his hands over his face. Han wouldn't even entertain the thought for a few hours before splitting? Maybe – maybe he just didn't understand what they were fighting for. He shared an exasperated look with Leia as she spoke to the captain through the comm.

There was time to work on Han, make him

see how important he could be in the fight. But first . . .

Luke leaned towards the viewport, resting his arms on the back of Chewbacca's chair. He was trying to absorb the jungle, the temples, the signs of power generators and laser defenses, all in one deep gulp rather than letting them warm him slowly, the way a solar panel took in the sun.

Luke bit his lip, not wanting to embarrass himself by asking Leia a million questions at once. Especially not when she had gone quiet and seemed lost in her thoughts. Of course. To her, this setting was typical, wasn't it? She was used to being in the thick of the fight. Luke was going to have to work not to show exactly how green he really was. The leaders of the Rebellion would never let him fly if they knew how small his world had been the day before.

Play it cool, he ordered himself, leaning back in his seat. *Don't think about how they'd probably prefer someone older, with more flying time under his belt. Someone like . . . Han.*

Who was still acting like he didn't care if anyone

in the Rebellion lived or died as long as he got his credits. Luke let his frustration rise before stamping it out. He was as good a pilot as Han. He just needed the chance to prove it.

The *Falcon* settled softly on a cleared patch of soggy mud, sinking the last few centimetres. Leia waited only long enough for Han and Chewbacca to start the shut-down procedures before she stood, smoothed her hair and dress, and made her way back to the droids.

Luke stood and followed her back through the ship, towards the hatch. "This place is something else."

"The Rebellion likes to use preexisting structures on remote planets. It makes us harder to track if we can pick up and leave at any moment," Leia explained, leaning against the hatch door. "These temples were built by the Massassi race thousands of years ago, and they're still standing. Hard to believe."

Hard to believe was right. Most structures on Tatooine lasted only a few years before they were buried by dunes or blasted by sandstorms. Had he ever seen something so old?

Luke's next question was interrupted by Han and Chewbacca coming down the ship's hall.

"All right, let's get this over with," Han said, checking the straps on his holster. "Looks like there's a nice welcoming committee coming out to meet us."

Leia put her hands on her hips. "Is that why you're checking to make sure your blaster is charged? Why don't you wait here and I'll have the money brought out to you. That way you don't have to waste any more of your *precious* time with our lost cause."

Luke was surprised to see that Han glanced over at him, frowning, before responding. "I'd like to check the place and make sure that . . . well, I mean, can't a guy protect his investment? I want to see the money loaded myself."

"Fine. Anything to get you moving faster," Leia said, hitting the button for the hatch. For a moment, Luke was afraid she'd jump down into the mud just to get away from the captain, instead of waiting for the boarding ramp to deploy.

"Have we arrived, Master Luke?" Threepio shuffled up behind him, Artoo repeating the question in a low pattern of beeps.

"We sure have," Luke said, resting a hand on Artoo's domed head and looking down at the little droid. "Didn't think you'd make it, did you?"

"Safe haven at last!" Threepio cried.

"Yeah, we'll see about that," Han muttered, waving Luke and the droids forwards. "These temples look one strong gust of wind away from crumbling into dust."

And Han thought *Luke* was overly critical? Luke stepped out of the cool, temperature-controlled ship and into a wall of moisture and heat. The air actually clung to his skin, climbing up his arms and neck like the thick green vines on the temples. By the time he made it down the ramp, his tunic was sticking to his shoulders and back, as if he'd run a mile under a scorching sun.

"Makes you miss the dry heat back home, huh?" Han said.

"No," Luke said. "I'd never miss that place. Not for anything."

Two transport speeders were parked a short distance from the ship. At the sight of Leia striding towards them, a man jumped out. "Your Highness! Thank the heavens!"

"It's good to see you," Leia said, when Luke and the others had caught up, "but time is of the essence. We need to download the information off that astromech droid. Where's Commander Willard?"

"Waiting for you inside the Great Temple."

The second transport speeder bucked slightly under their combined weight, but they all managed to squeeze in. Wedged between Han and the furry mountain that was Chewbacca, Luke had to lean way back to see the jungle as it streamed by in shades of lush green. Flowers bloomed in every colour, dripping from the trees, carpeting the ground. Every one of them seemed to strain out of the shade of the trees, towards the sunlight filtering through the dense canopy. The chirping of bugs and – oh, wow, *birds*! Birds that were *singing* rather than just picking the meat off old bantha carcasses. Were there other animals up in the trees? Luke had the unsettling feeling they were being watched, but it might have just been the guards stationed up on the platforms poking out of the jungle.

Instead of stopping at the base of the crumbling stairs leading up into the Great Temple, their driver brought them around back, to where a long hangar door had been installed. Luke slid out of the seat, crossing his arms over his chest to hide how much his hands were shaking. *Play it cool. . . . Play it cool. . . .*

The damp heat was just as smothering inside the hangar as outside, but there was so much more to distract him from it. Sparks showered down from fighter ships as technicians worked on them. Pilots milled around in orange jump-suits. There were droids everywhere. Between the metallic banging of ships being hammered back into their proper shapes and engines being tested, Luke couldn't hear himself think. The smell of oil and gas was everywhere, filling his chest.

He *loved* it.

It was everything he had pictured, and still it was also somehow *more*. Now Luke had to keep his arms crossed over his chest just to stop himself from bolting over to the cluster of men and women in orange jumpsuits, weaving through the towering fighter ships. They were incredible pieces of work, and that they'd clearly been banged up a bit in past fights only made them more beautiful in Luke's eyes.

That one, he thought, passing a ship with a long body and four laser cannons mounted on its wings. *That one's going to be mine.*

Ben was right. There had to be some kind of bigger force at work, guiding his life. Because if he'd gone off and entered the Academy, he wouldn't be there now, and where he was – that felt *right*.

"Nice collection of tech you've got here, Princess," Han said. "Anything that wasn't built before you were born?"

Leia spun on her heel, her eyes flashing again

as she rounded on Han. Luke whirled to face him in disbelief. Was he blind? The place was incredible! The energy in the hangar alone could have powered an entire fleet.

"You're so high on yourself and that hunk of junk you call a ship that you'll never understand that every victory we've had is due to the hearts of our pilots and their support on the ground," Leia said coldly. Han stood head and shoulders over her, but he might as well have been facing down a Star Destroyer. She somehow made herself seem that big, that terrifying.

Han stared at her in shock. "If all you have to stand up against the planet-blasting battle station are a bunch of bleeding hearts, you guys are in more trouble than I thought."

"Leia! Princess Leia!"

Whatever response was on the tip of Leia's tongue fell away when she heard her name. A middle-aged man with greying hair rushed up to them, his tan coat flying out behind him. Luke cast a covert eye over the man, trying to figure out his rank. Leia filled in the blank.

"Commander Willard!" Leia threw her arms around him. The man looked momentarily overcome with emotion.

"When we heard about Alderaan, we were afraid that you were . . . lost, along with your father," he said. "How are you holding up?"

"We don't have time for our sorrows, Commander," Leia said, pulling away from the circle of his arms. "I have no doubt the Empire is tracking us here."

He nodded grimly as he looked among Han, Chewbacca and Luke. "Is General Kenobi with you? Your father mentioned you'd seek him out after intercepting the plans."

Luke looked down at the mud-splattered toes of his boots, swallowing something hard and painful in his throat. Was it always going to be like that? Someone would just say Ben's name and it would feel like a punch to his throat?

Han clapped a hand on his shoulder and gave it a squeeze. Luke barely felt it.

He should be here, too, Luke thought, glancing

around him again. Ben would have been thrilled to see everyone working together. He was the one they really needed, not some young rookie dazzled by the sight of repair droids.

"General Kenobi was killed, Commander," Leia said, glancing at Luke. "He bravely sacrificed his life so we could escape the Death Star."

Chewbacca made a small mournful noise.

"The Death Star?" Commander Willard repeated. "They held you there?"

She nodded. "We'll be able to give you our observations of what we saw inside, but the important thing is that the technical readouts are on this R2 unit. We need to have the technicians download it so we can start analysing it immediately. It might be our only chance of defending ourselves when the Death Star comes into Yavin 4's orbit."

It was like Leia had dropped Commander Willard in the middle of a sandstorm. He suddenly looked very lost and more than a little afraid. Luke would have felt sorry for him if it hadn't been so obvious they were unprepared. Yes, they had ships. And pilots, too, by the look of it. All they seemed to be lacking was faith.

"We're badly unprepared for battle, Your Highness. Perhaps we should evacuate instead? Here – " Commander Willard motioned to two nearby technicians. "Take this droid into the command centre and download any information he has about the Death Star."

The two women accompanied the droid away as Commander Willard led the group farther into the temple. Luke was jostled as streams of Rebels pushed up and down the hall around them, all of them in a hurry to get somewhere. He wanted to go where they were going. He wanted to get to work and stop standing around, arguing.

"There isn't time," Leia said. "Commander, if we fail to stop the Death Star now, other planets will be annihilated."

"I understand that, but we're short staffed on pilots, trained or otherwise."

Leia looked right at Luke. "Well, you have at

least one more right here," she said, motioning towards him.

Luke was so shocked at how quickly the topic had come up, he almost choked on his own spit. He practically shouted, "Yes! I can fly!"

"A crop duster, maybe," Han scoffed, "but one of these snub fighters?"

Luke turned towards Han, glaring. So, what? The fight against the TIE fighters hadn't proven he could handle himself in battle? Or that he was at least a fast learner? Luke knew the hardest part of getting in the cockpit would be convincing every-one else he was ready for it, but for some reason he'd expected Han to believe in him.

Chewbacca shoved at Han's shoulder, but the captain ignored it.

"He's fast on his feet and has amazing reflexes," Leia insisted. "He mounted the rescue for me in a matter of moments – and . . ." She turned back to Luke. "You got us across that bridge without blink-ing an eye, remember?"

Luke ducked his head, trying to hide the flush

spreading across his face. While they were on the Death Star, after they had been separated from Han, he'd managed to lead Leia right into some kind of large airshaft. The bridge had already been retracted, the controls blasted out by laser rifle fire, creating a distance between the two doors that was too far to jump. Luke had hooked some of the rope from his utility belt on to one of the rafters, said a little prayer, and swung them both across.

"We wouldn't have gotten off the Death Star if Han and Chewbacca hadn't been there to help," Luke said, rubbing the back of his neck. "I didn't do it alone."

"Han?" Commander Willard looked confused. "Oh – the captain here."

"Yeah," Han said. "The captain. A real pleasure to meet you and all, but I'm going to skip ahead in this story to the finale. I was hired by Luke and this General Kenobi to shuttle them to Alderaan and promised a reward for bringing everyone here. I have no interest in your revolution, just in getting what I'm owed. I believe the number was seventeen thousand credits."

Commander Willard's skin went a chalky white.

"Han!" Luke could have throttled him for being so rude. He really couldn't wait a few hours to bring up money?

"We don't keep that sort of money lying around," Commander Willard said. "And this is . . . we need every cent to keep up our operations."

"I'm willing to accept the amount in precious metals if you don't have the credits on hand," Han said, crossing his arms over his chest. "Come on, pal, you don't want word to get around that the Rebellion can't honour their debts, do you? No one would be willing to do business with you."

"We do, but . . ." Commander Willard looked at Leia again, clearly confused. He'd been expecting an ally, if Luke had to guess, another new recruit. Luke was surprised at how bitter his own disappointment tasted; some part of him had hoped that Han would change his mind when he saw what the Rebels were up against.

But there was still time to try to convince him.

Luke couldn't understand a word of what Chewbacca said to Han next, but the past day had taught him to read the Wookiee's moods by his tone and expression. And Luke thought he might actually have an ally in Han's copilot.

"Give him whatever he wants," Leia said stiffly. The look she shot Han could have incinerated half the Death Star. "The sooner he gets it, the sooner he's gone."

That was exactly what Luke was afraid of.

CHAPTER SIXTEEN

LUKE HADN'T REALLY expected them just to assign him one of their fighters – X-wings, they were called, because of the way their wings were situated on either side of the cockpit – but he also hadn't expected a full-fledged test.

"You said you have some piloting experience?" The technician accompanying Luke seemed irritated to have been pulled away from his work. He hadn't even had a moment to wipe the grease from his face before striding over at Commander Willard's order.

"Some," Luke said. His T-16 skyhopper wasn't nearly as large as an X-wing or half as well equipped. But he could figure it out. He hoped. Maybe.

Yes, he thought, forcing himself to stand up straighter. *Yes, you can figure it out. Nothing to it. Just try.*

"Eh, well, we're sending out pilots who barely know to use the joystick to steer, so you can't be that much of a lost cause."

That was . . . not reassuring. Luke mopped at the sweat collecting on the back of his neck. Maybe Han was right and the situation was a lot more desperate than Luke had thought.

"Are you running the test?" Luke asked.

"No, I just set it up. One of the Red Squadron – those would be the X-wing pilots, bunch of hotshots and quick triggers – will come over and oversee your test."

Luke nodded, his nerves trilling inside his stomach. He needed to get a grip.

The simulator was tucked away in one of the far corners of the hangar. It looked like the interior of an X-wing cockpit had been lifted out of its shell and hooked up to a large monitor. Luke's heart about jumped out of his chest with excitement at the sight. A chart had been strung up on the wall beside it. A list of names – the pilots, Luke realised – and their scores on the simulator.

A small table and computer had been set up nearby. A dark-haired man wearing a rumpled orange jumpsuit was bent over the table, studying something on the screen.

"Wedge!" the technician called. "Here's your new recruit."

When the pilot turned around, Luke stopped in his tracks. He'd been painfully aware of how young he was compared with the middle-aged pilots hanging around the ships, watching him pass. But this pilot looked even younger than he was!

A grin broke across Wedge's face as he stuck out a hand towards Luke. "Wedge Antilles. Nice to meet you."

Luke remembered a half second too late that he was supposed to shake the pilot's hand. "Luke Skywalker."

"Good luck," the technician said to Luke, not bothering to offer any words of wisdom before he jetted away, back to his repairs.

"So . . . what's the deal here?" Luke asked,

running his hand along the back of the simulator's seat. "How do I pass?"

"Eager to get up into the stars, huh? I know that feeling." Luke didn't doubt for a second that Wedge did. He felt himself relax but couldn't tear his eyes away from the machine.

"The simulator is set to full combat mode. There's no *passing*, not exactly," Wedge said, leaning back against the table. "This computer right here will measure things like your response time, your shooting accuracy and, you know, how long you manage to stay in the fight before being shot down."

"I'm not going to get shot down," Luke told him, crossing his arms over his chest.

Wedge laughed. "All right. I like that spirit. Let's get you set up."

Luke practically leapt into the cockpit seat, not caring for a single second about what Wedge thought. He settled back against the old cracked leather, taking a deep breath as he buckled himself in.

"Er . . . you don't need to do that," Wedge said. "You aren't leaving the ground. It's all a simulation."

"I want it to feel as real as possible." That was the only way to really prove he was ready.

"Whatever you say." The pilot handed him a large white helmet with a yellow visor and Alliance decals all over it. "This will pipe in sounds. Just a warning, real battle is about a hundred times louder."

"Got it." Luke slipped the helmet on, adjusting the chinstrap. His hands were shaking a little now as he fumbled with the clasp. Everything was riding on this test. If he failed . . . well, Luke refused to be grounded for good. But it wouldn't help the Rebellion if he had to stay out of this fight and wait to be trained, hoping the Death Star didn't blow them all into dust in the meantime.

Wedge leaned into the cramped cockpit space. "You steer with the joystick, the proton torpedo switch is the button at the top, lasers are – "

"I got it," Luke huffed. "Just start the simulation."

Holding up his hands, Wedge backed away and

turned to the computer. Luke took a deep breath, filling his chest with the hot fuel-tinged air. The screen in front of him blinked once, twice, three times . . . then a battle exploded around him.

There were TIE fighters screaming in his ears, zooming across his screen so quickly Luke couldn't track them with his eyes. He didn't realise the simulator was equipped for shock and movement until he took his first hit of enemy fire; the cockpit rattled him so hard he thought it might have knocked his brain loose. The simulated g-forces as he rolled his ship out of the way made his bones feel as if they were stretching under his skin. He drove the joystick down, panic catching him by the throat and squeezing. The simulator made the dive feel real. Luke's stomach lurched with the suddenness of it, but he couldn't focus on the feeling for long. A TIE fighter appeared on the screen, and before he could react, he slammed right into it. A fireball overtook the image of space, only to be replaced by blackness and two words:

SIMULATION OVER.

The words burned worse than any sun. Luke sat back again, shocked and sickened at how badly he'd blown his test. Literally.

"At least you took out one Imperial ship when you went!" Wedge said cheerfully. He leaned into the cockpit again.

"I . . . don't have this," Luke said. How *stupid* could he have been to think it would be anything like the flying he'd done back home? The T-16 seemed like a toy in comparison. He was going to throw up. He really was.

Wedge didn't laugh. "Hey, Luke, it's all right – "

"I want this," Luke interrupted, hating the desperation he heard in his voice. "I want this more than anything. I've wanted this for as long as I can remember, and I can't even make it ten seconds?"

"Hey, you made it thirty seconds," Wedge pointed out. "That's nothing to sniff at, believe me. The first time I tried the simulator, I was down in less than ten."

"Really?" Luke couldn't believe that. Wedge's

name was at the top of the high scores chart! "Then how . . . ?"

"I practised and *listened* to the advice I got from the old vets. You didn't let me finish before," Wedge explained. "I was going to walk you through the different controls and systems. You're eager. I get it. But no one here expects you to have flown something as complex as an X-wing. It's not so hard once you get the hang of it, but you have to give yourself a few minutes to do it, OK?"

Luke nodded, feeling a fresh wave of embarrassment. "Sorry . . . about before, I mean. I should have listened."

He had proven all of Han's smug put-downs about his flying abilities right. That stung a bit more than he wanted to admit. It was hard not to feel a little foolish.

Wedge waved him off. "Nothing to be sorry for. It's something we all learn. I think you're going to be an amazing pilot, really. Half of it is confidence, so don't lose what you have. Let's clear out those results and start over, OK?"

This time, Luke swallowed his eagerness and pride and paid attention as Wedge pointed out all the controls, half of which he hadn't even noticed in all his scrambling to keep the X-wing flying. He asked questions and concentrated when Wedge explained slight variations in the thrusters and the difference between relying on yourself to fly and giving the controls over to the astromech droid at the back of the ship so you could focus on shooting.

"I'll be honest," Wedge said. "The droids tend to have a better response time with evasive manoeuvres, but sometimes instinct is the only thing that keeps you flying."

Luke nodded, setting his jaw as he absorbed all the information. Looking at the controls again, he began to make connections to the simpler ones he had used hundreds of times in his T-16. The ships weren't *that* different when it came down to it. He was finally feeling energised, not overwhelmed, at the prospect of the additional mobility and fire-power of the X-wing.

"See?" Wedge said. "You do know your ships! Can I give you one last piece of advice?"

"Yes!" Luke said. "Please."

Wedge rested his arms on the edge of the cockpit. "The time you stay in the fight matters less to Commander Willard than the readings and results he gets on how calm and composed you are. The simulator is designed to be impossible to beat. You're supposed to struggle and get shot down. In a real battle, you have an entire squadron backing you up. But the only way to improve as a pilot is to constantly come up against the impossible and push yourself to the limits. We all use the simulator to do just that. So just concentrate on keeping your cool and trust your instincts, OK?"

Trust your instincts. Luke ran the words over and over in his mind. Ben had told him the same thing as he trained with the lightsaber.

He reached for that settled feeling he'd obtained on the *Millennium Falcon* as he listened to Ben's musical voice telling him about the Force, how it wouldn't abandon him, how he could always rely on it. Using the sword had just *clicked* from that point on. If he could find that place again, Luke thought he could do more than just hang in the simulator for a few minutes.

"OK," he said. "I think I'm ready to try again."

"Good!" Wedge crossed back over to the computer and typed something in. He gave Luke a thumbs-up. When he was ready, Luke returned it.

He could do this.

He wasn't going to let his dream crash and burn.

The simulator went through its series of blinks again, counting down to chaos. This time Luke was prepared for what he'd see. The moment the battle came into view, he switched on his targeting screen and went to work.

Use the Force. Ben's voice whispered in his ear. *Reach out for it.*

Luke didn't know if that was what he was doing, but he felt his death grip on the joystick ease, something warm filling him at his centre. He was aware that he was aiming, firing, shooting. At some point he must have switched over to manual control of the ship, because he was rotating the joystick faster and faster, zipping in and out of explosions and clusters of Imperial ships. Avoiding them came as easily as avoiding Beggar's Canyon's sharp edges and deadly turns. The cockpit rattled around him as he took some fire, but he rolled the ship, a feeling of exhilaration, of total lightness, lifting him higher and higher and higher until he felt almost giddy. It was how he had felt the first time he successfully threaded the spindle of rock, the Stone Needle, back in Beggar's Canyon. He clicked into the moment.

All too soon, he saw how the simulator had been rigged against the user. For every TIE fighter he shot down, two more appeared. Soon it became just a matter of numbers. Not even the most skilled pilot could have lasted long against forty enemy ships.

SIMULATION OVER.

Adrenaline left his blood thrumming in his veins, even after he removed his helmet and sat back. He was dimly aware of a sound to his left

– clapping. Wedge and three other pilots in orange jumpsuits were hooting and cheering for him.

"Incredible!" one of them said, helping Luke down out of the cockpit. "You beat Wedge's record!"

Luke flushed again. "Sorry about that . . . ?"

"Don't be sorry!" Wedge said. "Stars, I'm just glad you're on *our* side. What did I tell you? You're a natural!"

His body was trembling a little, late catching up to the strain he'd subjected it to in trying to keep up with the pace of the simulator. The fatigue felt weirdly good; it meant he'd done something right and gone all out in the process. "Only because you helped me," he replied.

"When you write your autobiography, be sure to include that, OK? 'I owe everything to Wedge Antilles'!" Wedge and the other pilots laughed. One of them wrote Luke's name at the top of the score chart, and Luke felt pride wash over him.

But he wouldn't let himself celebrate yet. He wrung his hands in front of him, looking among their faces. "Do you think I passed?"

One of the older pilots, his hair flecked with grey, looked at Luke, eyes shining. "Commander Willard will review the results, but I think it's safe to start fitting you for a jumpsuit. That is, if you still want to join our squadron?"

Luke thought his heart might explode in his chest. He kept his arms pressed tightly against his sides to stop himself from throwing them around the other pilot.

"There's nothing I want more."

CHAPTER SEVENTEEN

ETWEEN GETTING Commander Willard's official OK to fly and finding himself a flight suit and helmet, there wasn't time for Luke to find Leia or Han to tell them the news. The pilots from both squadrons, Red and Gold, were summoned to the large war room for a briefing. Luke figured that they must have already gone through the technical readouts on R2-D2, and he told Wedge as much as they entered the enormous briefing area.

Luke had been schooled at home by his very patient aunt and therefore had never been inside a classroom. But he imagined that the war room was set up the way a lecture hall might be. Rows of seats led down to a large electronic wall display, where Commander Willard stood with another man Luke didn't recognise. It felt very formal, official in a way that made Luke walk a little taller, push his shoulders back. He only hoped he didn't stand out as a rookie as much as he thought he did. Every now and then a new pair of eyes would drift over, and he'd feel himself being sized up.

I just have to prove myself to them, too, Luke thought.

"That's General Dodonna," Wedge said as he led Luke through a line of feet and legs to get to two empty seats at the centre of the row. "He's a brilliant tactician. He was so good in his service to the Empire they picked him to be one of the first captains of a Star Destroyer."

"Got it," Luke said. Another thought occurred to him. "Was most of the Alliance in the Imperial forces at some point?"

Wedge set his mouth in a tight line. "Not everyone. Some of us joined to right the wrongs they inflicted on us and the people we love."

Luke let the subject drop, knowing that poking at exposed wiring never got you anything but shocked and burned. He scanned the room, his ears picking up on snippets of quiet conversations. His back went straighter as Leia and a small group of older men entered and took seats near the projector screen. Luke tried to catch her attention, but the princess was so focused on her conversation with the older gentleman to her right she didn't look up.

The murmuring dropped into silence as General Dodonna stepped up to a small podium, and the screen behind him flashed to life. Looming large, sketched out in lines, was the technical blueprint of the Death Star.

"Wow," Wedge said. "Is that thing as big as I think it is?"

"Bigger," Luke said quietly. Sometimes he had a hard time wrapping his head around just how enormous the battle station was.

"Welcome, everyone. I'll get right to the point," General Dodonna said. "We have analysed the plans provided by Princess Leia and believe we have developed a strategy for destroying the battle station known as the Death Star."

Luke leaned forwards in his seat, hands clasped. They'd already come up with something? Probably not a second too soon, if Leia's theory about the battle station tracking them back to the Rebel base was right.

"The Death Star is heavily shielded and carries firepower greater than half the starfleet's. Its defenses have been designed to withstand a full assault by an enemy army. But while it's easy to see a large fleet of cruisers and destroyers and hold back a tide, we believe a small, one-man fighter should be able to slip through the outer defenses."

The leader of the Gold Squadron stood up slowly. "Pardon me for asking, sir, but what good are snub fighters going to be against *that*?"

"I'm getting to that," General Dodonna said, clicking through to the next slide. The new schematic showed a cross section of the Death Star. "The approach will not be easy. Pilots will need to manoeuvre straight down this trench and skim the surface of the battle station until you reach this point."

Why that point? Luke wondered. It looked like any other part of the surface.

"The target area is only two metres wide. It's a small thermal exhaust port, right below the main port. The shaft leads directly to the reactor system." The screen changed, showing a demonstration of two torpedoes entering the shaft and travelling down its length to the enormous energy reactor at the centre of the Death Star. "A precise hit will start a chain reaction in the core, turning it into a bomb, causing the battle station to implode."

There was a moment of silence before the room broke out in cries of disbelief. The general continued, undaunted. "Only a precise hit will set up a chain reaction. The shaft is ray shielded, so you'll have to use proton torpedoes."

Luke nodded, processing the news with outright relief. So there *was* a chance. It might have been only a two-meter-wide chance but a chance all the same. They could do it.

"That's impossible, even for a computer," Wedge said, shaking his head.

"It's not impossible," Luke said, loudly enough for the others to hear. The pilots sitting around him turned in their seats, pinning him with looks that ranged from curious to confused. It maybe wasn't the best way to introduce himself to the rest of the Rebellion, but there were bigger things to worry about than making a good first impression. A negative attitude would keep the pilots grounded long enough for the Empire to destroy everything they'd built. "I used to bull's-eye womp rats in my T-16 back home. They're not much bigger than two metres. And I didn't have any kind of targeting programs. We can do this."

"Well . . . better than a few centimetres, right?" Wedge said. The pilots around him nodded.

"Come on," Luke said, smiling. "I was doing that when I was thirteen. You guys have decades of experience between you, right? Prove it!"

Garven Dreis, the leader of the Red Squadron,

laughed. "That's true. Can't let a kid show us up, can we?"

Luke turned back to General Dodonna, who was studying him from the front of the room. Beside the general, Leia was smiling, her hands clasped in front of her. The tone of the murmurs around Luke shifted, rising on that small bubble of optimism.

"We've received reports that the Death Star will enter the system within the next twenty minutes," General Dodonna said. "Man your ships, and prepare to deploy immediately. Good luck!"

"That's our cue," Wedge said, standing. "You ready?"

"Yeah – " Luke searched over the heads of the other pilots for Leia, but she had already slipped out of the room – back to the command centre? There was still time to seek her out for a good-bye, but the flow of energy and bodies out of the room was carrying him straight back to the hangar. He let himself go with it, the hum of anxious excitement from the others feeding his own. Luke was nearly bouncing in his boots by the time he met up with C-3PO and R2-D2.

"Master Luke!" the protocol droid cried. "Is it true Artoo will be accompanying you?"

"If that's all right with Artoo," Luke said, grinning. The little droid's head spun around as he squealed, lights flashing. "I'll take that as a yes."

But nothing could have brought Luke's mood crashing down faster than seeing Han and Chewbacca loading small boxes onto the *Millennium Falcon*. Their reward. Payment the Rebellion could hardly afford to lose. As they worked they ignored everything happening around them, including the dirty glances the pilots were shooting their way.

"All flight troops, man your stations." The announcement faded under the hustle and bustle of the technicians and flight crews running around. *"All flight troops, man your stations."*

Luke pushed his way through the workers, dodging the carts and transports zigzagging around him. It was stupid to feel so crushed at the thought of Han leaving, but Luke had already lost so many people over the previous few days. Luke had just wanted his friend to see what Luke had seen in him.

"So you got your reward and you're just leaving?" Luke called, trying to keep the hurt out of his voice. He had never expected Han to stay for him, exactly, but how could Han leave seeing what the Rebellion was up against?

"That's right, yeah. I got some old debts I've got to pay off with this stuff. Even if I didn't, you don't think I'd be fool enough to stick around here, do you?"

Luke shook his head. No, Han was no fool. If he could just get over himself, he'd be something great.

"Hey, why don't you come with us?" Han said. "You're pretty good in a fight. We could use you."

Chewbacca backed up his statement with an enthusiastic roar.

Luke's frustration flashed into anger. "Come *on*! Why don't you take a look around? You know what's about to happen, what they're up against. They could use a good pilot like you. You're turning your back on them!"

"What good's a reward if you ain't around to use it?" Han shrugged but seemed to be looking everywhere but at Luke. "Besides, attacking that battle station ain't my idea of courage. It's more like suicide. Can't you see that? You're throwing your life away for people you've just met!"

"This might be hard for you to understand, but I believe in what they're trying to do. I'm proud to be part of it, no matter what happens."

Luke waited for Han to say something, but the captain kept his head down, steadily passing boxes to Chewbacca.

"All right." Luke threw his hands up in the air. Trying to get through to Han was about as effective as trying to walk through a wall. "Well, take care of yourself, Han. I guess that's what you're best at, isn't it?"

He turned to go, only to be pulled back around by Han's voice.

"Hey, Luke . . ." Han said, a faint smile on his face. "May the Force be with you."

Even though there was a real possibility Han was making fun of Luke again for jumping into Ben's lessons, Luke chose to take his words as sincere. "Thanks. See you around?"

There was nothing more to say. Luke made his way towards the row of X-wings being prepped for flight and was surprised to see a familiar face waiting for him there with R2-D2.

"Thought I'd let you go without wishing you good luck?" Leia said, with a rare smile. "I heard you did amazingly well on your test."

Luke suddenly found the ground incredibly interesting as heat flooded his cheeks. "I guess."

"What's wrong?"

He sighed. "Oh, it's just Han. I don't know. I thought I could change his mind."

Putting a hand on his shoulder, Leia said, "He's got to follow his own path. No one can choose it for him."

She stood up on her toes and kissed Luke's cheek. "Fly well. I'll see you when you get back."

He managed a small smile and a wave as she went to meet with General Dodonna.

Luke took a deep breath, twisting around to look up at his ship.

"Luke? *Luke!*"

He spun, searching for the source of the voice. It couldn't be – there was no way – Biggs Darklighter, his best friend, came barreling across the hangar towards him. He burst into thrilled laughter at the sight of Luke staring at him, dumbstruck. "Luke! I don't believe it! How'd you get here? I was out on patrol – wait, are you going out with us?"

Luke accepted his enthusiastic hug and returned it with one of his own. He should have known! A short time before Luke's life had been upended, Biggs had made a surprise visit back to Tatooine from the Imperial Academy, stopping by to see his friends at Anchorhead.

Luke couldn't lie; he had been jealous of Biggs

when he escaped Tatooine for the Academy, but the sight of his friend in a full uniform had choked him up with more than a little envy. Biggs was out ahead of him. Some part of him had accepted that it would always be that way between them. They were an unlikely pair of friends. Everyone said so. The Darklighters owned twenty moisture farms to Uncle Owen's one. Biggs had always had the very best of everything growing up – clothes, landspeeders, a new skyhopper each time another model was released. He'd never held it over Luke's head or made Luke feel like he was something less. But . . . Luke had always sensed how different their lives were, and it wasn't until Biggs had gone and left him behind for the Academy that he had realised how different their futures were, too.

But on that last trip to Tatooine, Biggs had pulled Luke aside from their little group of friends – Fixer, Camie, Deak, and Windy – and confessed something to him: he was going to bail on the Academy and join the Rebellion. Luke couldn't believe he hadn't put the pieces together until that moment.

"Oh, man, do I have some stories for you. . . ." Luke was grinning so hard his entire face ached. This was incredible! Of all the people to run into . . .

Biggs knocked a fist into Luke's shoulder. "I've got to go get aboard. Listen, you'll tell me your stories when we come back. All right?"

Biggs started jogging for a nearby X-wing.

"I told you I'd make it someday, Biggs!" Luke called after him.

His friend held his arms up in the air, echoing the triumph Luke felt. "You did, all right. It's going to be like old times!"

Luke gripped the ladder of his ship, starting the short climb up. His heart was racing like crazy – the way it had each time his skyhopper had clipped a wing passing through the narrow canyon. The crew chief had to wave his arms to get Luke's attention.

"This Artoo unit of yours seems a bit beat-up,"

the man called, gesturing to where the droid was being lifted into the socket at the back of the ship. "Do you want a new one?"

"Not on your life!" Luke shouted back, swinging his legs into the cockpit. "That little droid and I have been through a lot together." He switched on the comlink to the droid. "You OK back there, Artoo?"

The cheerful whistling he got in response was enough to make him grin again as he clipped his helmet on. The glass-and-metal canopy was lowered over him and sealed into place. Fiddling with his heavy leather gloves, Luke watched the last gasp of activity below. As he went through the ignition sequence, a soft, familiar voice whispered in his ear: *Luke, the Force will be with you.*

He just about jumped out of his skin in surprise. That was – it was like on the Death Star. That was Ben's voice.

No. That was his mind playing games with him.

Luke leaned back against the seat, closing his eyes. It was happening. It was all finally happening.

He had R2 at his back, he had Wedge's lessons, and now he had Biggs out there flying with him.

He was ready.

CHAPTER EIGHTEEN

⟐

THEY SHOT UP through the atmosphere, winging into space in a tight formation. The Y-wings fanned out around Luke's squad as they rounded Yavin 4 and came face to face with the Death Star.

"Woah!" Luke couldn't tell which pilot had let his surprise slip, but Luke didn't blame him. The first time he'd seen the battle station, his insides had twisted into tiny little knots. Now he just felt like he was soaring, and he was chasing the feeling full throttle. The X-wing was nothing like flying his skyhopper, or the simulator.

"All wings report in," Red Leader called.

They moved down the roster. Biggs chimed in as Red Three, Wedge as Red Two.

"Red Five standing by," Luke said when it was his turn.

"Lock S-foils in attack position," Red Leader said.

Luke reached up and flicked the switch that would unfold the wings of his ship, locking them in the X position.

"We're passing through their magnetic field," Red Leader said, his voice over the comm crackling with interference.

"Doing OK, Artoo?" Luke asked, adjusting his controls. The X-wing began to bounce, as if it had hit a small invisible patch of asteroids. The droid chirped back, and the X-wing translated his message on a nearby screen: ALL SYSTEMS GO.

"Switch your deflectors on," Red Leader said.

Yikes, right — that would be helpful. Luke quickly did as he was told, glancing up through the canopy. Half the Death Star was shadowed by the planet Yavin, the other half illuminated by the soft glow of the nearby sun. Luke's hands clenched the controls as his breath caught at the back of his throat.

Now that they were closer, Luke could make out the thousands of tiny structures lining the battle station's surface, the twinkling lights on the different control stations and towers. The other ships spread out around him, silently filling the endless space around them.

"Red Leader, this is Gold Leader."

"I copy, Gold Leader."

"We're starting for the target shaft now."

"Copy that. We're in position. I'm going to cut across the axis and try to draw their fire."

Two groups of fighters peeled off from the others. Luke steered his ship down towards the Death Star, following his squadron into a sudden spray of laser fire from one of the space station's surface-mounted cannons.

"Heavy fire!" Wedge reported.

"I see it," Red Leader said. "Stay low, everyone."

There was a system to the attack – who would take the first shot at the exhaust port, who would fall in line behind if the pilot couldn't finish his or her run. Gold Squadron would make the first attempt, with the other squadron covering them and trying to draw fire away from their ships. But Luke knew that when it came down to it, *anyone* could and should take the shot if he or she had it – including him.

He threw his X-wing down into a sharp nose-dive, firing at one of the laser cannon towers. The structure burst into a fireball far bigger than he expected, and as hard as he yanked back on his controls, the ship wasn't pulling up fast enough to avoid it. Terror slammed into his chest.

"Luke, pull up!" he heard Biggs cry.

The X-wing shuddered as it passed through the edge of the explosion, emerging with singed wings.

"Are you all right?" Biggs called over the comm.

Luke swallowed the lump in his throat, shaking off his fear. "I got a little cooked, but I'm OK. This is Red Five. I'm going back in."

"Watch yourself!" Red Leader barked. "There's a lot of fire coming from the right side of that deflection tower."

"I'm on it," Luke shot back. He spun his ship into another rapid dive, his concentration narrowing on the target. He fired along a stretch of the Death Star's surface, wiping out small radars and towers as he went.

The Death Star blurred through his window as he picked up speed. To his right, he saw Biggs make a similar dive into a field of domes and antennae, narrowly avoiding return fire from the battle station.

Then there was that sound – that telltale screech. Luke craned his neck to confirm what his target screen and ears were telling him. TIE fighters. Dozens of them.

"Enemy fighters at point four," Red Leader called. Luke was vaguely aware of the control officer back on Yavin 4 repeating the information, asking for an update. He tried to imagine what the battle looked like to those below, whether their hearts were pounding as hard as his was.

"Red Three!" Red Leader's voice interrupted Luke's thoughts. Red Three was Biggs. Luke searched the surface of the Death Star, trying to locate his friend. "You've picked up an enemy fighter . . . watch it!"

"I can't see it!" Biggs called back. *Where is he?*

Luke saw the TIE fighter on his friend's tail, just as Biggs dropped closer to the surface.

"He's on me tight. I can't shake him. . . . I can't shake him!"

Biggs changed direction so quickly, Luke found himself flying upside down for half the dive to reach his friend. "Hang on, Biggs, I'm coming in!" Luke glanced over his shoulder at his astromech. "I need more speed, Artoo!"

Whatever the droid did, it gave him another burst of power. When Luke had the TIE fighter in range, he didn't hesitate. He blew it into a thousand pieces, scattering the enemy ship to the stars. "Got him!"

Instead of relief, Biggs just sounded more panicked. "Pull in! Luke . . . pull in!"

"Watch your back, Red Five!" Wedge chimed in. "There's a fighter above you, coming in!"

In a move that would have broken his skyhopper in half, Luke forced his X-wing into a steep climb. His ship's tail got a wallop of a blast from the TIE fighter, but he didn't lose control.

"Status?" Red Leader called.

"I'm hit, but not bad," Luke said. There was another sudden explosion behind him as a TIE fighter he hadn't seen was sent crashing into the Death Star. He caught a glimpse of Wedge's face through his canopy.

"Thanks, Wedge," he said, shaken.

"No problem!"

"More enemy fighters coming in!" Gold Leader reported. "We're making our run!"

"Copy that," Red Leader said.

As if that weren't enough bad news, the base back on Yavin 4 sent another terrifying update over the comms: "Death Star will be in range in five minutes."

OK, Luke thought, holding his breath. Five minutes was still plenty of time. They'd need only a few seconds, anyway, to get the actual shot off. Now it was just a matter of getting close enough to do it.

"Switching to targeting computer!" Gold Leader said.

"They're coming in too hot!" Gold Two said. "Gold Leader, I can't – "

Luke knew without confirming it on his screen that Gold Two's ship had been destroyed. Luke adjusted his course, swinging around to support the run.

"Stay on target, Gold Leader," Red Leader said. "Loosen up!"

It was too late. Even with Luke's helmet visor down, the flare as Gold Leader's ship was blown apart stung Luke's eyes. An ache rippled through him as he scrambled to think of what to do next. Gold Five moved into place to take the shot.

"Red Leader, this is Base One," General Dodonna's voice came over the comm. "Keep half your group out of range for the next run."

"Copy, Base One," Red Leader said. "Red Five, take Red Two and Three. Hold up here and wait for my signal to start your run."

"Understood," Luke said, scanning the skirmish breaking out beneath him. Sweat worked its way down his face and made his flight suit stick to his back.

"Keep your eyes open for those fighters!" Red Leader said.

"There's too much interference! I can't get a read on my screen!" That, from Red Ten, who was trailing behind the squadron leader.

"Red Five, can you see the enemy fighters from where you are?"

Luke pulled himself forwards in the cockpit, looking down through the canopy. "No sign of any . . . wait! Coming in point three-five!" Three TIE fighters were dogging the others, racing along the vein of the Death Star. The one at the centre was slightly different from the others. Its wings curved at the edges instead of standing up straight.

"I see them now!" Red Ten said.

"I'm in range," Red Leader said. "Target's coming up!"

Luke's breath caught in his chest again. So

close . . . They were so close. . . .

"Just hold them off a few more seconds!"

"I can't hold them!" Red Ten's panic ripped through what little calm Luke had managed to keep. Red Ten's X-wing exploded in a shower of sparks just as Red Leader fired his proton torpedoes at the exhaust port.

"It's a hit!" Red Nine cried.

"Negative . . ." Red Leader sounded like he was on the verge of tears. "It didn't go in. It just hit the surface. Red Five, prepare to make your run."

"Hear that, Artoo?" Luke said.

AFFIRMATIVE. READY.

"Me too." He switched his comm back over to the others. "Wedge, Biggs, close up. We're going in full throttle – "

There was a horrible scream as Red Leader crashed into a nearby tower, his ship taken down by the fire from the strange TIE fighter. Luke saw it all happen through his window and felt some of his hope shrivel up.

"We lost Red Leader," he reported back to base,

though he had a feeling they already knew.

"Proceed with your run, Red Five," General Dodonna said. "You're in charge."

"Right behind you," Wedge said.

"Luke, at your speed will you be able to pull out in time?"

Despite everything, Luke managed a small smile. "It'll be just like Beggar's Canyon back home. Don't tell me you're scared now!"

The three X-wings powered forwards, blasting every nearby structure they could. The Death Star's defenses returned fire, but Luke was flying past, catching only bits of the explosion. The ride got rougher, bouncing him around, rattling his brain inside his skull. *Hold it together, hold it together* – a shot from one of the towers clipped him, jerking his ship. The sound of alarms filled the cockpit.

"Artoo . . . that – that stabilizer's broken loose again! See if you can't lock it down!"

He saw a shower of sparks out of the corner of his eye.

"Blast it, I'm hit!" Wedge cried.

Luke gritted his teeth. "Get clear, Wedge. You can't do more good back there!"

They had already lost so many of their fighters. They couldn't afford to lose Wedge, too.

"Sorry!" Wedge sounded agonised. He was a fighter to the core, Luke knew, and he would have gone down swinging if Luke had let him.

Luke was in the trench now, racing along the same path Gold Leader and Red Leader had taken. His target screen flashed to life as he pulled it down to estimate the distance to the exhaust port.

"Artoo, try to increase the power again!"

The rattling grew worse. Pops and flashes of explosion lit either side of him.

"Hurry, Luke, they're coming in much faster this time," Biggs warned from behind him. "I can't hold them!"

Luke tried looking back over his shoulder again as he felt the engines flare with new life. *Good job, Artoo,* he thought. *Now –* "Hurry up, Luke!" Biggs shouted. "Wait – !"

The force of the explosion nearly sent Luke

hurtling nose first into the surface of the Death Star. His grip on the controls slipped, just for a second, as shock and pain and anger and a thousand other emotions rocketed through him.

Biggs was gone.

CHAPTER NINETEEN

***

LUKE WAS ALONE.

The realisation sliced through him, cutting him up inside. It hurt even to breathe.

Biggs . . . it just . . . it didn't feel real – how could Biggs be gone, when Luke had only just found him again?

Just like his aunt and uncle. Just like Ben. Even Han and Chewbacca had left.

"Status, Red Five!"

Luke shook himself, trying to break out of his stupor. His X-wing leveled off as he regained full control. Tears tracked down his cheeks, but he wiped them away against his shoulder. This was a battle. This was their one chance. He couldn't let the others down by just – just packing it in and giving it all up, no matter how much his chest felt like it was about to cave in on itself.

"Still on track for my run," he said. His whole world became the targeting screen. As the TIE fighters raced up behind him, he rolled right and left to avoid their fire. A sudden chill overtook even his pulsing anxiety as he risked a glance back towards the TIE fighter with the angular wings. He felt like death itself was chasing him.

Don't think about that, he ordered himself. The yellow crosshairs on his targeting screen steadied as the exhaust port came into focus.

Use the Force, Luke.

There it was again! Ben's voice filled his mind like a cloud of warm smoke. The Death Star's surface raced under him. He was hearing what he needed to hear – a comforting, familiar voice. Luke turned back towards the targeting device and adjusted it.

Let go, Luke.

Again! He shook his head, but it was like Ben was sitting behind him, placing a calming hand on his shoulder. *Let it go, Luke. . . .*

If the Force was as limitless as Ben had said, if it was with him in every moment . . . why couldn't Ben somehow be reaching across it to encourage him? He knew what Ben was asking him to do. Turn off the targeting screen. Trust his instincts. But this was it, his one shot. Yavin 4 was minutes away from being destroyed, and the Rebellion along with it.

Hadn't Red Leader tried to use the targeting system, though? It hadn't worked for *him*, even though the system had been perfectly calibrated. Luke turned the thought over in his mind, his pulse speeding as fast as his ship. And then there was that moment on the *Falcon*. Luke had been blinded and still managed to deflect the blast from the remote. That should have been impossible. But maybe that's what Ben had really been trying to tell him: the impossible could become possible if he was just willing to trust himself and the Force.

Luke, trust me.

Grim determination pooled in the centre of Luke's chest. He took a deep breath, closing his eyes and reaching, reaching, reaching for that place of warmth he had felt on the *Falcon* and in the simulator. It was like slipping into a refreshing stream after being caught under the pounding sun for too long.

Luke reached up and flipped a switch. The targeting screen drew back with a *click*, clearing his field of vision.

"Luke, this is Base One." General Dodonna's voice crackled over the comm. "You've turned off your targeting computer. What's wrong?"

"Nothing," Luke said, feeling the last bit of tightness in his chest ease. "I'm all right – "

A burst of laser fire from the TIE fighter with the angular wings engulfed R2, sending sparks flying. Luke was sure he could hear the little droid wailing as he looked back over his shoulder, trying to assess the damage.

"I've lost Artoo!"

"The Death Star is in range of the planet," General Dodonna warned.

The trench narrowed slightly as Luke raced

towards the exhaust port, his hand steady on the controls, his thumb flicking up the cover over the launch button for the proton torpedoes. He felt like he was being carried along by a powerful stream. But instead of being afraid, he was sure of himself, sure that he could succeed.

Another explosion from behind him momentarily rocked his focus.

"*Yahoo!*" A new voice joined the fray, overpowering the surprised sounds from Base One and the other pilots. A smile stretched across Luke's face.

"Han!" Luke yelled.

The *Millennium Falcon* was cruising behind him and had destroyed two of the TIE fighters and sent the third one with the odd wings spinning off into space. Luke could hear Chewbacca roaring in victory in the background.

"You're all clear, kid!" Han said. "Now let's blow this thing and go home!"

Luke turned back to the task at hand, his finger over the trigger for the torpedoes. When the feeling came, a strong nudge from some invisible energy force, Luke slammed his thumb down on the trigger and fired.

CHAPTER TWENTY

— ✦ —

LUKE WATCHED the twin bursts of light disappear into the exhaust port and pulled his X-wing up and up and up out of the trench. The sigh he released shook his whole body. Luke blinked in disbelief, looking down again. It felt like he was coming out of a dream as he soared up towards the stars.

"Great shot, kid!" Han cheered. "That was one in a million!"

One of the other pilots confirmed the hit to the base on Yavin 4 in that single quiet second before everything changed.

Luke knew that the moment would be imprinted on his memory forever. The way the ring of pure energy and fire blew out from the centre of the battle station, ripping it apart into nothing more than shreds of metal and dust. The pressure of the detonation rocked the X-wing, sending it bobbing. Just as quickly, his flight smoothed out again and calm returned to the galaxy. The terrifying giant was gone, and with it the weight of fear that had been pressing down on Luke.

Remember, he heard Ben say, *the Force will be with you . . . always.*

And it would be. Luke saw that now, feeling, for the first time, that all these parts of himself – the farm boy desperate to escape, the Jedi trainee, the Rebel Alliance's new piloting recruit – had fused. He saw the future spread out in front of him, opened wide.

Luke's descent into Yavin 4's atmosphere was filled with the cheers and cries of the officers and staff in the control room. He brought his X-wing down low over the jungle, cutting through the thick mist until the temples finally appeared in front of him. He waited his turn to pull into the hangar, falling in behind the remainder of the Red and Gold Squadrons. By the time he made it inside and initiated the landing procedures, the whole of the Rebellion had flooded in to greet the pilots. He had never been so relieved to see all their faces.

Luke scrambled to unhook his straps and push the canopy up. He tossed his helmet on the seat and was halfway down the ladder before he took his next breath.

"Luke!" Leia ran towards him, a blur of white pushing through the crowd. "Luke!"

He somehow managed to catch her as she slammed into him, laughing. He swung her around in a huge hug, setting her down just as Han came up behind them, grinning from ear to ear. The captain didn't resist as Luke pounded his back.

"I knew it!" Luke said, punching his shoulder for good measure. "I knew you'd come back!"

Han shrugged. "Well, I wasn't gonna let you have all the credit!"

Chewbacca growled behind Han, giving the captain a little shake.

"All right, all right, and because we wanted to make sure you got out of this mess in one piece!"

Han said. "How does it feel to be a hero?"

"Oh, my! *Artoo!*" At Threepio's distressed voice, Luke spun on his heel. In all the excitement, he'd somehow managed to forget about the droid who'd had his back. A technician was lowering R2-D2 to the ground carefully to avoid damaging him further. His white-and-blue body had been scorched nearly black. Wiring stuck out from his joints like climbing weeds, and one of his small arms had been blown off.

"Oh, no!" Luke said, rushing over.

"Artoo!" C-3PO wailed. "Artoo! Can you hear me? Say something!" The protocol droid turned to the mechanic. "You can repair him, can't you?"

The technician nodded. "We'll get to work on him right away."

"You *must* repair him! Sir, if any of my circuits or gears will help, I'll gladly donate them!"

"He'll be all right," Luke said, resting a hand on the protocol droid's shoulder. Facing the others again, he was surprised to see Leia smiling up at Han.

"I knew there was more to you than money," she said.

"Don't tell anyone," he said with a wink. "Wouldn't want to ruin the surprise, Your Worship."

"*Leia*," she insisted, rolling her eyes. "Just Leia."

Luke felt a smile tug at the corners of his lips as Wedge came up behind him and punched his shoulder. "Nice shooting!"

"Couldn't have done it without you!" Luke had to shout to be heard over the songs and cheers that had broken out again. Wedge let himself be swept up into the group, pumping his fists in the air.

For a moment, Luke hung back from the others, leaning against his ship. The atmosphere was humming, brimming with the excitement of everything they had accomplished. Still, he couldn't miss the holes – the empty places where people should have been. The squadron members who hadn't lived to see the Empire brought to its knees. Biggs.

Ben.

Uncle Owen and Aunt Beru.

His father.

You were right, Luke thought, smiling again as Chewbacca hugged Leia and then lifted her right off her feet. *Ben, you were right.*

He had felt the Force. He didn't fully grasp it yet, and he knew there was so much more he needed to learn, about himself and his capabilities. But now he knew that the loved ones who had left him weren't so far away after all. He could feel them nearby, like beams of sunlight breaking through the clouds.

When Luke closed his eyes, he saw Tatooine's twin suns sinking into a violet glow, burning on the horizon and casting the sand in brilliant gold. He'd been so determined to leave, he'd refused to see the beauty of his home and everything it had done to make him who he was.

"Hey, kid!" Han called, waving Luke over. "You ready for a real celebration?"

The crowd was moving out of the hangar, headed deeper into the Great Temple. No doubt, Luke thought, to dig into what supply of food and drink they had left.

Kid. Luke snorted. Maybe Han would always call him that. Maybe the older pilots would think he was just a rookie hotshot who got lucky. Maybe Leia would always think he was just a simple guy from a planet at the farthest edge of the galaxy, not refined or brilliant or particularly charming.

But Luke knew now he was so much more – and that he had so much farther to go.

This time, no one was going to hold him back.

EPILOGUE

EPILOGUE

WHEN THE SUN ROSE golden and bright the next morning, it wasn't just on the ancient temples of Yavin 4 but on a new galaxy – one shining with possibilities. As the three figures stepped up to the entrance of the Grand Temple's throne room, each was overwhelmed by the towering stone walls and ceilings carved with intricate patterns. The jungle was in full bloom, coating the damp air with a rich floral scent.

The soldiers of the Rebellion had donned their finest, helmets and boots gleaming as the sunrise filtered through the ceiling above in shafts of light. They stood at attention on either side of the long aisle. Three figures stepped up to the entrance of the great chamber. Luke fidgeted in his new clothes, clasping his hands behind him to hide the way they shook, just a little. He relaxed at the sound of Han's soft whistle next to him. Chewbacca urged them forwards, to where a figure in white waited for them. Celebratory music began, and at the first cue of the trumpets they started down the steps and towards the front of the throne room.

Leia struggled to hide her smile as they strode towards her, wanting it to mean as much to them as it did to her. The Rebellion had opened their arms to her, ushering her into a new home, giving her new purpose in helping guide their course.

Near where she stood, two droids – perhaps the true heroes in all this – had been polished and shined and given a place of honour at the front of the ceremony. A repaired Artoo began to bounce on his three legs, whistling in delight as Han, Chewbacca and Luke came to stand before Leia.

The medals had been placed with care on a tray. Leia turned, picked up the medals and, one by one, placed them over the three heroes' heads.

They turned back towards the soldiers and

officers and took a bow together. The room erupted in cheers.

The princess, the scoundrel, the farm boy.

The senator, the smuggler, the dreamer.

The Rebel leader, the captain, the pilot.

More than what they believed of themselves.

More than what others saw of them.

And, together, a new hope for the future.

ACKNOWLEDGMENTS

MY THANKS first and foremost go to Michael Siglain, Emily Meehan, and the entire team at Disney for giving me this unbelievable opportunity. It's been a dream of mine for . . . well, pretty much my whole life not only to become a writer but to write the kind of *Star Wars* book I grew up reading. I am totally humbled and awed by the responsibility – *thank you!*

Sending blue milk and Wookiee cookies to all my new friends at Lucasfilm, especially Rayne Roberts, Pablo Hidalgo, Leland Chee, Frank Parisi, and Jen Heddle. Your passion and dedication to maintaining our (let's be honest) favourite galaxy is so inspiring, and it's been an absolute pleasure and honour to work with you!

Adam, Tom, and Tony – I've loved getting to know you all and geeking out together! Thanks for showing me the ropes of the MG world. I'm so proud to be part of our awesome (if I do say so myself) little team . . . and I'm *still* laughing about Downtown Disney.

To Susan Dennard and Sarah J. Maas, my favourite bounty hunters: I would never have gotten through this without you two. It's just that simple. Thank you for *everything* – your feedback, your excitement, and your belief.

And, finally, I owe everything, even my love of *Star Wars*, to my family. It's been an incredible journey over the years, and I'm grateful for it every day. Mom, thank you for encouraging me to try my hand at this and helping me wrangle all of the many emotions that came with working on something so close to my heart. (And, you know, for bringing that Gamorrean guard figure home from your trip!) Dad, I am a writer today because you brought this wonderful story into my life and led us on so many adventures. We miss you and love you, and we know that the Force will always be strong with you.

AUTHOR BIOGRAPHY

ALEXANDRA BRACKEN was born and raised in the desert of Arizona, where she spent her childhood waiting for someone to give her a lightsaber and send her to save the galaxy. When that didn't happen, she jetted back east to attend the College of William & Mary, where she studied English and history. She now lives in New York City, the closest she could get to living on Coruscant. Her favourite *Star Wars* character is Salacious B. Crumb. (Just kidding – it's Princess Leia.)